Lexia, an ordinary human, catches the eye of a werewolf who tries to force himself onto her. In order to save her, she's placed into a mate bond with a pure-blooded werewolf who could never possibly love her. At least, that's what he says. But when lines blur and feelings become a bit too real, he knows he's in trouble.

River where the Moon Rises
Copyright © 2024 Wie-aam Adams
ISBN: 978-1-4874-3570-7
Cover art by Martine Jardin

Published by eXtasy Books Inc

Look for us online at:
www.eXtasybooks.com

River where the Moon Rises Under the Moon Duet 1

By

Wie-aam Adams

PROLOGUE

Amaris.

That voice. It's so distinct that I can never mistake it for someone else. It's the voice in my head. The voice that whispers to me at odd times, the voice that calls out a name I can hardly call my own.

Amaris. That name isn't my own, yet it feels as though it belongs to me. It feels as though whoever the voice belongs to is being affectionate, and most importantly, it feels as though the voice is trying to tell me something, something important. But I have no idea what.

Lia tells me I'm imagining things, and the psychiatrist tells me I'm crazy.

I don't want to believe either of them, but the more the voice whispers to me, the more I start to think that I really am losing my mind. I want, no, I need help from someone who will be open to new and slightly odd ideas as to what this is. In the world we live in today, where supernatural creatures such as werewolves and ghouls exist and live among us, one would think that people would be more open to such issues as this, but if anything, it's made them even more closed off and even afraid.

Humans fear these supernatural beings, and I know that if I even try to find a supernatural reason for hearing the voice in my head, I'll be shunned. I may even be written off as worse than creatures whose eyes glow and who turn into beasts at night.

All I can do is remain silent about what I hear, for who knows what may happen to me if I don't.

CHAPTER ONE

"This is not a good idea."

Lia rolls her eyes at me, her fingers gripping my forearm as she pulls me down the dark street. I'm not sure what time it is right now, but it's most likely after midnight already. Luckily, I told my father I would be sleeping at Lia's place tonight. Otherwise he would have been furious. It was already a struggle to convince him to let me stay at a friend's house, and hopefully he won't get so drunk tonight that he forgets he gave me permission.

Although, I'm pretty sure he'd be livid if he knew where we are, well, heading to right now. I'm not sure why, but I let Lia convince me to let her take me to the tattoo studio downtown, and now, as we near the studio, anxiety creeps in and wraps itself around my bones.

When we finally stop in front of the studio's entrance, I pull back, grabbing Lia's attention. "This is really not a good idea, Lia. My father will kill me, and you know that I'm not exaggerating when I say that."

"Look, let's just have fun for once. You're always bailing out on doing things because you're afraid your father won't approve," she says with an exasperated sigh.

I can't help but stare at her with wide eyes. But then again, how can I expect her to understand when she doesn't know my home situation? All she thinks is that my father is strict.

"We can get it done somewhere where he won't see. Problem solved."

"I don't know, Lia . . ." I trail off, pursing my lips in

2

uncertainty.

"Come on. Just this once, Lexi." She practically begs, staring at me with pleading eyes. Sighing, I nod in defeat, and she cheers, knowing that she's always had me. She gives me no chance to even think of changing my mind because she pushes open the door and pulls me inside. The studio is exactly what I thought it would be—a simple desk at the front with pictures of tattoo designs littering the walls. The arms of the woman at the front desk are littered with tattoos, and she's wearing obsidian black contacts that covers the entirety of her eyeballs, as well as a medusa piercing and gauged ears.

I swallow when her dark orbs focus on me. It may be presumptuous of me, but her appearance makes her look scary, so I'm hesitant to walk forward, but Lia nudges me, pulling me from my thoughts with an unimpressed look. I let her do all the talking, avoiding having to look at the woman by staring at the tattoo designs on the walls instead.

They're all so detailed, with intricate lines and strokes. Most of the designs look like they require a lot of space, and I'm not about to let a stranger fill a big part of my body with ink. The woman leads Lia and me to a back room and knocks on the door twice before leaving us. A rough voice mutters out a throaty, "Come in," and she pushes open the door, revealing a room with a similar look as the front of the studio.

A man sits on a roller chair, and I'm almost immediately intimidated when he twists around to face us. There's not much difference in his appearance to the woman's. However, I think it's the fact that he's much bigger physically that scares me. He looks like he can crack my skull open with his bare hands.

"Take a seat," he says, gesturing to the leather seat beside him. Lia eagerly sits and produces her cell phone from my pocket. She shows him a picture of what I'm assuming to be the tattoo that she wants. It seems like she's been thinking about this for a while now. The entire time the tattooist does her tattoo, I look away, the mere buzzing sound of the machine making me feel anxious.

I'm not sure how long I remain standing there, and it's only when I hear Lia call out to me that I finally bring my attention back to them. My eyes immediately find her tattoo. It's a simple tattoo, three birds fluttering their wings on her collarbone. It reminds me of a tattoo I saw in a movie once. The tattooist gestures for me to sit down when Lia stands up, and I swallow, hesitantly sinking into the leather seat.

"What do you want today?" he questions, peeling the black latex gloves off his fingers. His question has me stunned. Everything's happened so fast. At the beginning of tonight, getting a tattoo was the last thing on my mind, so now that he's asking me what I want permanently inked onto my skin, I'm at a loss for words. "If you don't have a specific design you want, I can show you some that we have available."

I nod at his suggestion, not having a clue about what to get. He takes a thick flip file from the table into his hands and places it on my lap. I flip it open, and Lia is by my side as we flip through all the pages. But just as I'm about to flip to the next design, a drawing at the bottom of the sleeve catches my attention.

It's a simple design, with a glittering silver moon and a tiny black wolf howling beneath it. I'm not sure why, but I immediately feel drawn to it. It's almost as if the drawing speaks to me, and as if fate, the voice in my head whispers to me *This is the one.*

The words the voice whispers to me have me thrusting the flip file towards the tattooist. I point at the design, and he nods, although I don't miss the way his eyebrows furrow slightly in confusion, and I know why. A human getting a tattoo of a wolf is unheard of, especially since even though they live among us and don't harm us, we still fear them. And the fact that they look just like us makes us even more anxious. I could be dining with a werewolf, and I wouldn't even know.

"Where do you want it?" he asks, slipping on a clean pair of gloves.

Almost immediately, my hand flies to the side of my neck, just below my ear. He nods and gestures me to lie down. I do, gripping Lia's hand tightly. She smiles down at me, squeezing my hand in encouragement. I suck in a breath when the machine touches my skin, even though it's not even on yet.

I can do this.

When the buzzing sound of the machine fills my ears, I close my eyes tightly shut and squeeze Lia's hand. Then the needle pierces my skin.

I try not to scream at the pain that immediately travels throughout the area where he permanently tattoos my skin. I'm not sure how much time passes by, but by the time the buzzing stops, I slump into the seat, all energy drained from my body.

"It's done, Lexi," Lia whispers to me, and my eyes flutter open, my vision slightly blurry.

"It looks beautiful," the tattooist says, smiling proudly as he stares down at my neck. I nod, releasing a breath. I would hope so, considering how painful that was.

"Thank you so much. I just know she'll love it when she sees it," Lia says.

He places a patch on the fresh tattoo, telling me that I can take it off tomorrow morning. I nod, standing up from the seat, albeit with shaky legs. I'm never doing this ever again.

We leave the back room and proceed to pay, Lia insisting on paying since she's the one who convinced me to get a tattoo even though I didn't originally want one.

"I can't believe I just got a tattoo," I say as we walk out of the studio.

"How does it feel? I bet rebelling against your father feels delightful," she says with a laugh, stuffing her wallet into her bag.

"I'm not so sure about that. I'll see how I feel after seeing the result tomorrow," I say with a shrug.

"It already looks great raw, so it'll look even better once it's healed.

I can only hope she's not just saying that so I don't freak out. The weight of what I have done hasn't sunk in yet, so for now, I don't even think about how I'm going to hide this from my father tomorrow.

"But why did you get that design?" she questions.

I was waiting for that question. She surprised me by not saying anything when I first chose the design, so I just knew she would ask why I got it afterwards. "I liked it," I say with a shrug.

"But just remember, that's going to remain there forever. I don't want you to regret getting a wolf.

I know that she's saying that for my sake. She's afraid of what people may say when they see it. They may even accuse me of being a werewolf because of it, but I don't care. If I'm going to get something permanently inked onto my skin, I want it to at least be something I like. I don't want to have to think about what others may say. As long as I like it, then I don't care.

"I won't regret it, Lia," I say, and then she stops.

"How do you feel about werewolves?" she suddenly questions, her tone turning serious. "Now that I've thought about it, we've never talked about the topic before. You know how I feel about them, yet I have no idea how you feel."

From the moment we met, Lia has expressed how she feels about supernatural beings, specifically werewolves. She fears them but thinks that they're sexy and wants to spend the night with at least one of them for the experience. Her view of them isn't very accurate, considering the fact that neither of us has ever seen a werewolf in real life and wouldn't know, but she swears they're sexy. It's just the gut feeling she gets, and all I do is indulge her, knowing that arguing with her is no use, especially when I can't agree or disagree with her.

"I don't know how I feel about them." It's true. I've never sat down and thought about them before, so I'm not sure what to think or feel when it comes to them. Of course, just like every other human on this planet, I fear them and their power, but I don't have any personal feelings towards them.

"So if I were to show up with a werewolf boyfriend, you wouldn't mind?"

My eyebrows furrow. "Is there something you've been hiding from me?" I question, narrowing my eyes at her. She immediately shakes her head.

"It's not like that. It's just . . . there's been a rumour circling the school recently," she says.

"What rumour?" I question. It's not surprising that there's a rumour that I don't know about. Unlike Lia, who wants to know everything, I'm quite okay with not knowing everyone's business. I actually prefer it that way.

"Well, they've been saying that we're getting transfer students on Monday," she says.

"And?" I question.

"Well, rumour has it they're, you know . . . werewolves."

Werewolves? Werewolves are transferring to our school? "Why?"

She shrugs her shoulders.

"I thought that humans and supernatural beings are separated for a reason. You know, so that no one gets killed."

She nods, folding her arms across her chest. "I guess this is their way of trying to get us to get along."

I shake my head. Werewolves going to the same school as humans?

That spells trouble.

CHAPTER TWO

The sun hitting my face wakes me.

Stretching out my limbs, I roll over onto my side. Well, at least I try to, but Lia has her entire body lying on top of mine, the weight of it preventing me from being able to move my own body.

"Wake up, Lia," I say, patting her bottom. "We have to get up for school."

She merely groans in response, but luckily, she rolls over onto her stomach, allowing me to finally breathe. I get to my feet with a sigh, my hand rising in the air to shade my face from the harsh sun rays. It's going to be very warm today. I can tell that much without even having to go outside first.

Then there's a knock on Lia's bedroom door, and it opens slightly, revealing her mom, Vanessa. "Oh, I see you're already awake. You only have half an hour to get ready before you have to leave."

I nod. "I'll wake Lia."

Vanessa sends me one last smile before disappearing, closing the door behind her. My eyes find Lia's sleeping form on the bed, and I sigh. Waking Lia up from a deep sleep has always been quite the task, and usually I just leave her to wake up on her own, but if I don't wake her up myself today, we'll both be late for school, seeing as she needs a specific amount of time to get ready, doing her hair and a full face of make-up taking up most of the time.

"Lia." I try, but when she doesn't respond, I decide that there's no use in me merely calling out to her. Taking a deep breath, I jump onto the bed, landing right on top of Lia. She immediately groans at the impact, and I smile. Lying on top of Lia and basically suffocating her is the only thing that actually works in waking her up.

"Get off me." She groans into the pillow.

"Not happening. You have to wake up and get ready for school," I say, putting more pressure on her body.

"I don't feel like going to school today. I'll just skip it today." She groans again.

I sigh. How am I supposed to get her to get up now?

Then, as if it's the universe's way of helping me, I recall the conversation we had last night. "Really? Because if you stay at home today, you'll miss the werewolves."

Almost immediately, her head snaps up. "The werewolves?" she questions, as if she'd forgotten about them, and I just reminded her.

"Yep." I smile when her head turns to mine. "Unfortunately, if you stay at home today, you won't get to see those sexy werewolves today."

Suddenly she's sitting up, causing me to nearly fall off the bed.

"I have to go to school today. There's no way in hell I'm missing that," she says, determination evident in her voice. She quickly gets up from the bed, pushing her feet into her slippers and rushing out of the bedroom.

I can't help but laugh at the change in her, and all I had to mention was werewolves and sexy to get her to cooperate with me. She really has a simple mind.

Lia quickly finishes in the bathroom before returning to the bedroom to get ready while I make my way to the bathroom. The moment I'm standing in front of the mirror, my eyes find the patch on the side of my neck, and I'm reminded of the tattoo I got last night. I don't regret it, but I might once I rip the patch off and see the tattoo for the first time.

Taking a deep breath, I bring my hand to the patch and quickly rip it off my skin before I have a chance to hesitate. I look into the mirror, my eyes widening when I see how the tattoo came out.

I'm surprised. I'm not sure why, but I expected it to be a complete failure and flop as a sort of punishment for going against my father's will. But it's the complete opposite of what I expected. It looks just like the picture in the file, as if the tattooist pressed copy and paste. I dare even say that the actual result is better than the original design.

There's just something about this design, something special that has my mind and heart calling out to it.

"It's perfect," the voice in my head whispers.

"Is there a reason why you told me to get this one done?" My fingers move to trail across the tattoo inked onto my once untouched and bare skin. It may sound weird to others, but sometimes, on rare occasions, I communicate with the voice in my head. Most of the time, it's just me talking to myself, but at infrequent moments, the voice responds to me, even if it's merely with one or two-word sentences.

Just like the majority of the time, the voice doesn't respond, leaving me with unanswered questions. Honestly, ever since I got the tattoo of a crescent moon and wolf done, I've wondered why the voice advised me to choose this specific design. Usually for trivial things such as this, the voice doesn't interfere, and that's mainly why I decided to listen to the voice last night, because I know it wouldn't say anything if it wasn't important.

Shrugging off my thoughts, I take a quick shower before wrapping a towel around my naked body and heading back to the bedroom. Lia is busy applying foundation when I enter the bedroom, and I walk to the overnight bag I packed, zipping it open and pulling out my school uniform from it.

I drop my towel to the ground, not caring about the fact

that Lia can see my bare body since we've been naked in front of one another before and are comfortable with it. I slip into my underwear and school uniform, tugging my school skirt up my legs before tucking my white shirt into it. I slip into a pair of sneakers, not having worn actual school shoes since I started attending high school.

I move to stand behind Lia in front of the mirror—where she sits at her dresser—and I drag a brush through my wet hair, deciding to just let my hair hang naturally for school. When Lia is done with her make-up, we both head downstairs, deciding to skip on breakfast since we're running a little late for school.

Vanessa places a kiss on Lia's head as we leave the house, causing a little envy to slip in. I'd also had such a relationship with my mom in the past before she died from cancer. At times like this, I find myself wishing that I could go back to the time when she was still alive. I think a part of me knows that if I could go back, I would appreciate my mom a lot more than I did before.

"Oh, I'm so excited." Lia squeals when we reach the school gates, a skip in her step.

I roll my eyes at her, not even bothering to ask her why she's so excited, already knowing why. While she may be excited, I feel the complete opposite. I secretly hope that the rumour about werewolves transferring to our school is just that, a rumour. No matter how good-looking they may be, there's no hiding the fact that they're dangerous. Who knows what they may do to someone who accidentally crosses them? I can only hope I won't make a mistake if they do end up attending the same school as me because I'm really not looking forward to dying before I graduate.

I can be wrong in my judgment of them. However, it's understandable considering the power they have, the power that only they have.

"That's it. I have a plan." Lia suddenly announces, pulling me from my thoughts.

"What plan?" I question.

"I'm going to choose the hottest of the werewolves and seduce him. I mean, I don't think even he'll be able to resist me," she says, boasting and flipping her hair over her shoulder. She's not being conceited when she says that. It's no secret that men fall to their knees before Lia since she's quite the beauty, with her baby blue eyes and long, silky, dirty-blonde hair. She's the pretty one out of the two of us. I'm not ugly, but I'm just not considered extremely pretty when I stand next to her, with my shoulder-length golden-brown hair and hazel green eyes.

"Good luck with that," I merely say, walking past her.

I reach the classroom before Lia, taking a seat at my desk. Lia strolls into the classroom moments after me, sending her flirty smile to the boys she passes before coming to sit next to me.

"Why did you walk away?" She places her bag on the floor.

I merely shrug, keeping my attention to the front. The bell rings, and the teacher, Ms Blake, a petite woman with thin-rimmed glasses perched on her nose and hair always pulled back in a braid, comes walking in, her purse clutched firmly to her chest.

"All right. Good morning, everyone." She places her purse on her table. We greet her back, although with less enthusiasm than she had. "Right, we have new students today."

My heart stops. New students? It can't be . . . no way . . .

"It's them. I can feel it," Lia excitedly whispers, nudging me with her elbow. I can't share the same excitement with her. Here I was, hoping that it was merely a rumour, but now, not only is it not a rumour, but the transfer students are in my class.

Talk about bad luck.

"It's the werewolves."

"I told you it's true."

"I wonder what they look like."

Whispers erupt throughout the classroom, and I stare uncomfortably at the front, awaiting their arrival.

"I really hope they're hot, or else I'm going to be heavily disappointed," Lia says to me, a pout on her face.

I don't respond, intertwining my fingers on the desk in front of me.

"You may come in." Ms Blake announces, and then the door opens. Everyone leans forward in their seats, curious to see the werewolves. The moment a foot steps into the classroom, I avert my gaze down to the desk.

Almost immediately, the air in the room shifts. The power — I can feel it practically seeping out from their bodies. If there was ever any doubt that they're werewolves, all of it's vanished. With the powerful aura, there's no way they're human.

"Look up."

My head immediately snaps up at the voice in my head, my focus falling onto the werewolves. There are three of them, one with surprisingly gentle features, having short blonde hair and crystal blue eyes. The other has jet-black hair shaved into a buzz cut with honey-coloured eyes. He looks bored as he stands there, his hands stuffed into his pants pockets.

Then my gaze falls onto the one in the middle. He feels different. Everything about him feels different.

If anything, his aura is more powerful than the other two's. The power is rolling off him in waves. There's something different about the look in his eyes, too. It's almost as if he's seen so many things that I can't even begin to imagine.

Our eyes meet.

CHAPTER THREE

I can't look away.

I want to, but I can't seem to. It's as if something, or someone, has taken control of my body, and I can no longer do what I want. The werewolf . . . his gaze is unfaltering, his eyes staring deeply into mine even from a distance. His eyes, though, there's a certain glint in them, as if he's challenging me to look away first. Suddenly, as if his challenge has awakened something in me, I intensify my stare. He raises an eyebrow at me, appearing not to have expected that from me.

I'm not sure why he has any expectations, though. He doesn't even know me.

I want to examine him and graze my eyes over every inch of him. I'm curious that way, but as we stare deeply into one another's eyes, I realise that there's no chance for me to, not without breaking eye contact with him, and it seems like that's what he wants from me right now.

"What are you doing?" The sound of Lia's voice breaks me out of the moment, and my head instinctively snaps to hers.

It's only when I stare into her eyes instead of his that I realise I broke first. Staring at him in the periphery, I find him to be looking away now, too, but there's a quirk to his lips, a quirk that shows me he's satisfied.

Releasing a breath of frustration, I twist my body to face Lia. "Why? What is it?"

Surprise flashes in her eyes. "Woah, Lexia Leigh."

The fact that she calls me by my full name instead of just calling me Lexi, as she usually does, shows me just how surprised she is.

"Sorry. I was just surprised," I feebly say, releasing a breath.

She nods, although the slight furrow to her eyebrows doesn't disappear.

"And? Have you chosen a target?"

She nods, a smile appearing on her face as she points her finger to the front. "Him."

It's him. She chose the one in the middle, and I can see why. Physically, he's unmatched.

Now I take my time to really look at him, my gaze roving over every inch of him. He has thick and tousled golden-brown hair that splays across his forehead, a few stray strands falling into his chocolate-brown eyes that have a few golden specks in them. I can see them, even from a distance.

But he's big. Physically, he's big, muscles straining the school shirt he wears, and his tall height hovers over every-thing. He's a man.

"And? Do you approve?" Lia's question pulls me out of my thoughts.

"Huh?" I distractedly mutter.

"Do you approve of him?" she asks, pointing at the beast of a man.

"Well . . . I guess in terms of looks, he's not too bad," I half-heartedly mutter.

"Not too bad? Lexi, you need to get your eyes checked. Be-cause that" — she grabs my arms and turns my body so I'm looking at him — "is a man."

She's just voicing what I've been thinking. He really is a man, so how can he be a teenager? He has to be at least a few years older than us. There's no way he's eighteen.

"All right, so you may introduce yourselves," Ms Blake says.

"I'm Cole," the one with the buzz cut says, his voice low

and in monotone.

"Hi, everyone," the one with the gentle features greets, raising his hand in the air. I'm surprised by the cheerfulness in his voice. "I'm Gage. Nice to meet you all."

Then everyone's attention is on *him*.

"I'm Rykan."

Everyone gasps. His voice . . . it's so deep.

"Oh gosh. I'm in love." Lia gushes from beside me, flashing heart eyes at him.

Rykan. It tastes foreign on my tongue.

"Right, anyone have any questions for them?" Ms Blake politely asks.

"Are you werewolves?" a voice boldly pipes out from the back of the class.

Everyone's eyes are on them, awaiting their answer.

"None of your business." Cole answers, his voice stern and making the person shut their mouth.

"But don't you think we deserve to know? I mean, we're going to be in the same class for a year," Lia buts in from beside me

My head snaps to hers, my eyes wide. Her facial expression is nonchalant as she stares at them. I know why she's asking. She wants a steamy romance with a werewolf, and if it turns out that they're merely humans, she'll be heavily disappointed.

"Why do you think you deserve to know?" Rykan surprises everyone by questioning. The tone of his voice is accusatory and stern.

"What do you mean?" she asks, although I hear a slight tremble in her voice.

"Isn't this the same as blatantly asking you if you're a virgin in front of everyone?" he asks, and she gasps, her eyes widening at his words. And his mouth quirks. "And judging by your reaction, I'm guessing you're not."

16

"That's enough!" I blurt out, standing up in my seat.

"What?" he nonchalantly asks.

"You can't just say that!"

"And why not?"

"Because it's personal," I say.

"And asking us whether we're werewolves or not isn't?" he asks.

I freeze. All thought of what to say left my mind. He's right. He's got me with that.

"All right, guys. That's enough," Gage softly scolds. "We shouldn't get into arguments so early on the first day."

Rykan keeps looking at me as Gage speaks, his eyes slightly narrowed.

Then Gage turns to me. "I apologise for Rykan. He's not really good with words."

"You three can go to your seats now," Ms Blake says, cutting in, then clearing her throat awkwardly.

Rykan glances at me one last time before Gage pulls him and Cole to the back of the class.

"Are you okay?" I ask Lia, grabbing her arm.

"Huh? Yeah, I'm fine. He was just a little scary, that's all."

Lia's quiet throughout the rest of the lesson. Although I can see that she's clearly a little shaken up by the way Rykan spoke to her, I leave her alone.

When the bell rings, Lia is up from her seat. "I'll see you at lunch."

She's out the door before I can respond. Sighing, I get up from my seat, but just as I take a step into the aisle, I bump into something hard. When I look up, my eyes widen when my gaze meets Rykan's. Now that he's so close, I can clearly see the golden specks in his eyes. They strike me frozen for a few moments before I break out of it.

"Watch where you're going," he hisses, pushing past me.

I scoff, the next words tumbling out of my mouth without

control. "Bloody dogs."

He stops, his body tensing. My eyes widen, and my hand flies to my mouth. Did I just say that? What's wrong with me? I must have lost my mind. Even though it hasn't been confirmed if they really are werewolves, I'm screwed.

Rykan slowly turns to me, his eyes dark. "What did you just say?"

The calmness in his voice has me gulping. "Nothing. Did you hear something? I most definitely didn't."

It's a poor attempt at playing it off, but it's all I got.

"But I thought I heard —"

"She said she didn't say anything," Cole suddenly says, stepping in front of me. I'm surprised at his behaviour, to say the least, but I don't protest. He's helping me for whatever reason, and I'm not about to stop him.

Rykan's eyes narrow at Cole, but then Gage grabs his arm. "You're just being paranoid. Let's go."

Rykan allows Gage to pull him out of the classroom, and I release a breath of relief when he's gone.

Cole's eyes are on me. "Never say that again unless you want to lose your life."

Gulping, I nod, watching him as he walks out of the classroom.

"Are you okay, Lexia?" I hear a voice ask from beside me, and I distractedly nod, although, my heart racing in my chest tells me that I'm anything but okay.

Just when I told myself to stay out of their way, I called them dogs. There's nothing worse you can call a werewolf. Well, that and mutts. But this is bad. I'm probably on Rykan's hit list now, and I don't think anything will erase what just happened from his mind.

In simple words, I'm screwed.

Sighing, I trudge to my next class. When it comes to lunch, I'm not looking forward to going to the cafeteria, but Lia will most probably be waiting for me there, and after what happened this morning, there's no way I'm leaving her alone, especially when she can easily fall prey to those transfer students.

She's sitting at our usual table when I enter the cafeteria, and I quickly get my lunch before making my way over to her and sitting down next to her. The first thing I notice when I sit down is that she looks different from earlier, and the cheeriness has returned to her face.

"Are you okay?" I ask, and she nods, a smile appearing on her face.

"The transfer students were in my art class, and Gage apologised to me for Rykan," she says. "And I've decided to give up on my steamy fantasy with Rykan. He's too mean. I'll just have to find another werewolf."

"We don't even know if they *are* werewolves," I say, reminding her and placing a fry into my mouth.

"Lexi, they're werewolves, trust me," she says and leaves no room for questions.

Leaning back in my seat, I think about her words. She sounds so sure of herself that I can't do anything but believe her.

Then everyone in the cafeteria goes quiet, and something behind me catches her attention. I twist around in my seat and see the transfer students walking into the cafeteria. The air in the room becomes tense as everyone is unsure of whether they're werewolves or human. They don't seem bothered by everyone's stares as they quickly grab their trays and walk to the lunch lady, who stares at them with wide eyes and an agape jaw. Even she looks shaken by their presence. However, she quickly breaks out of her trance and dishes food onto their trays, albeit with shaky hands.

She looks beyond relieved when they walk away with their food, and I watch them as they take a seat at an empty table, which just so happens to be in the centre of the cafeteria and the only unoccupied table, as if the universe wants them to be at the centre of attention.

"Everyone's staring at them like they're some kind of beasts," Lia says.

"Well, if they are indeed werewolves, then I guess they are beasts." She merely hums in response, stabbing her fork into her lettuce.

"Hey, you dogs," a familiar voice yells out, capturing my attention. I look up to see a boy I know walking to them. Jackson, I think is his name. He's in the same grade as I am, although in a different class. He looks like a typical bad boy, with his jet-black hair, brown eyes, and all-black clothes every single day, no matter how hot it is, and an added feature to his bad-boy look would be his pierced ears.

The transfer students ignore him, remaining silent while eating their food.

"I'm talking to you," Jackson says in an entitled voice, kicking the back of Cole's chair. "Hey."

"What do you want?" Gage twists around in his chair to stare at Jackson.

"Well, I just wanted to know how long you're planning on hiding your true identities from everyone." Jackson stares at Gage with a taunting smile.

"I have no idea what you're talking about."

"Oh, please. I'm not stupid enough to fall for your lies."

"What do you want from us?" Cole speaks this time.

"What do I want from you? I want you to be honest and tell everyone here what you really are." Jackson gestures toward everyone with open arms.

They don't respond to Jackson. Even Gage looks like he doesn't know what to say.

"Just get lost," Rykan surprises everyone by saying.

Jackson laughs, throwing his head back, completely

unaffected by the bite in Rykan's voice. "Now that's not very nice, is it, Rykan?" His voice dropping a note as he says Rykan's name.

"Does it look like I care?" Rykan says.

"You know, I have a feeling we would be best friends if you weren't such an asshole," Jackson says. "Oh no, wait. Never mind. I don't think I would ever be able to be friends with a werewolf."

Everyone gasps at Jackson's words and, most importantly, him calling Rykan a werewolf. No one seems to notice, but I notice Rykan's clenched fist underneath the table. It's shaking, as if he's trying hard not to get up and punch Jackson. I don't blame him.

"Come on, Rykan. Just tell everyone the truth. It's not like everyone doesn't suspect you in the first place. Just confirm their thoughts," Jackson says, smiling tauntingly at him.

"Why don't you just stop? None of this is necessary," Gage says.

"Why don't you just get lost? You're not welcome here," Jackson says, and this seems to be the last straw because Rykan is up from his chair and grabs Jackson by his collar, clenching his fist around the material.

Jackson just looks amused. "Go ahead. Show everyone the kind of monster you are." He's daring them with a mischievous glint in his eyes.

"Rykan, don't," Gage softly says as he and Cole both stand up.

"Gage is right, Rykan. He's not worth it," Cole says, his eyes conflicted.

I can tell that he, too, wants to just hurt Jackson but holding himself back.

Rykan's entire body is shaking as he holds onto Jackson. He's angry, I can tell. Very angry.

"Go ahead," Jackson challenges.

Rykan looks like he's about to give in, and all I can think about is what's going to happen if they do end up fighting.

Nothing good.

I wish for them to stop. I wish for Rykan not to give into the urge. But I can see that he's slipping, and if no one does anything, there will be blood.

When Rykan speaks, his voice is deadly. "You're dead."

CHAPTER FOUR

Someone's going to die.

I can feel it. Barely thinking, I jump up from my seat and yell, "Wait!"

Rykan freezes, his entire body tensing. Then he turns his head, and his gaze meets mine.

"What?" he questions, and I gulp. Everyone's staring at me now, awaiting my response. I, however, have no idea what to say. I wasn't thinking when I yelled out, and now Rykan is staring expectantly at me.

"Um . . . well," I start by saying, biting my lower lip in thought, and then something comes to mind. "Where do you think you are right now? If you're going to fight, do it elsewhere."

I'm speaking in a bold voice. However, not knowing how he may respond makes me anxious. He may blow up at me, and that's the last thing I need right now.

"Lexia, stay out of this," Jackson says, and I'm surprised to hear him say my name. Why does he speak as though he knows me?

"Do you two know each other? Is that why you're doing this?" Rykan questions, and I vehemently shake my head.

"No. I don't know him," I say, holding my hands up in defence.

"Your fight is with me. Leave her out of it," Jackson says.

Rykan scoffs. "Who told you you can speak?" he says, his voice deep.

"Please stop this. It isn't worth it," I plead.

"And what would you know?" he questions, staring at me

with accusatory eyes.

He's right. I don't know anything. I look down, not knowing what to say to that. I have nothing I can say. Why did I even bother interfering? I should've just kept my mouth shut. Curse me and my mouth.

"Rykan, that's enough now," Gage says, his voice sounding serious for the first time since I've seen him.

Rykan sighs, his eyes fluttering closed as he tries to calm himself. When his eyes open again, they're empty and devoid of any emotion. He lets go of Jackson and takes a step back.

"Stop challenging him," Gage says to Jackson before grabbing Rykan by the arm. "Let's go."

When they're gone, I release a breath of relief before falling into my chair.

But within an instant, Jackson is by my side, his eyes dark as they stare down at me. "Never do that again."

Then he's gone.

When I arrive at home, my father isn't home.

Releasing a breath of relief, I ascend the stairs and head to my bedroom. I take a few minutes to unpack my overnight bag before taking out my books and starting on my homework.

By the time I'm done with all my homework, the sun is setting. I yawn, stretching out my limbs. The time has flown by, and I'm still in my uniform. I take a quick shower and slip into a pair of sweatpants and a tank top before heading downstairs. When I pull open the fridge, I realise that there's no food when I come face to face with emptiness.

Sighing, I grab my wallet from the table and leave the house, making my way to the convenience store. When I reach the store, I push the door open and immediately start searching for their ready-made sandwiches. Luckily, I find a chicken-mayo sandwich and grab it quickly before making my way to the front counter to pay for it.

The moment I'm at the front counter, I feel uncomfortable. The man, or should I say boy, stares at me, his eyes scanning up and down my body before he licks his lips.

"Will this be all?" he asks.

I nod, pulling out a note from my wallet, wanting to leave here as soon as possible. I don't like the way he looks at me.

"Here, take this. Free of charge."

He slides a can of soda my way, along with the receipt that I notice he has secretly written his phone number on. There's no way I'm going to be calling him, but I take it with a smile, thanking him for the free soda before making my way to the door. However, just as I reach it, a hand wrapping around my wrist stops me. When I turn around, he's right behind me, and I instinctively take a step back, my back pressing against the door.

"Is there something I can help you with?" I ask, clearing my throat.

"If you didn't notice, I wrote my phone number on that receipt. You'll call me, right?" he asks, smiling sweetly down at me. However, I know better than to fall for that. The look in his eyes tells me that this is anything but innocent.

"Of course." I lie, flashing him a smile.

"Well—"

Suddenly, the door is pulled open, and I fall back. I close my eyes as I await the impact of hitting the ground, but it doesn't come. Instead, my back hits a hard chest, and a hand touches my waist, balancing me as I fall.

My eyes flutter open, and they widen when they meet a familiar set of brown orbs. Surprise flashes in those eyes, him probably not having expected to see me here as I was to see him. For a moment, it's as if time stops, and all I can see, all I can feel, is him. However, the moment is quickly broken by the sound of a throat being cleared. It snaps me out of the moment, and I quickly look away, my eyes finding the boy. I quickly stand upright, my eyes widening slightly.

"Sorry," I softly mumble to Rykan, looking down at the ground. Without another word, I turn around and rush past him, my cheeks flushing with heat. That was embarrassing.

When I reach my home, I release a breath of relief. That relief is short-lived when my eyes meet my father's as I walk in. he's leaning against the wall beside the staircase, his arms folded across his chest as he stares at me with narrowed eyes.

"Where have you been?" he questions.

"There was nothing to eat, so I went to buy something at the convenience store," I say, clenching the sandwich in between my fingers.

"And you didn't think to get your poor father something, too?" he asks, tilting his head to the side. He's patronising me, and he's anything but a *poor father*. He's hardly a father. He then holds out his hand. "Give it to me."

Releasing a frustrated breath, I walk to my father and hand him my wallet.

He opens it and sifts through it before pulling out the few notes of money I have. "Is this all?"

I nod, staring down at the ground.

"Pathetic," he mutters before throwing the notes at me, the paper hitting my face before fluttering onto the ground. "How am I supposed to buy my whiskey tonight?"

I don't respond, not knowing what to say. He sighs, pinching the bridge of his nose.

"We have no choice then. You'll have to entertain my friends tonight."

My head snaps up at his words, my eyes widening. What did he just say?

"What?" I softly ask, unsure if I heard him correctly. He didn't just tell me to entertain his friends tonight.

"You heard me correctly," he says, as if he doesn't

understand the weight behind his words.

"No. I'm not doing that. I refuse," I say, folding my arms across my chest. Almost immediately, his eyes darken.

"Do you think you have a choice?" he questions.

"I'm not doing it."

He takes a step forward and grabs my arm, his nails digging harshly into my skin. "Yes, you will."

"No, I won't," I firmly say, and before I can even realise what's happening, his hand makes contact with my cheek, leaving a stinging sensation behind.

"How dare you speak back to me?" he barks, anger overtaking his features.

Tears form in my eyes, and I sniffle. He slapped me. It's nothing new, but it still hurts. Blinking, I wipe away a tear that's fallen and look up at him. "I'm not doing it."

He then grips the top of my head with his hand and pushes down, causing me to fall to my knees, my sandwich falling from my hand. Another tear escapes.

"I must have been too nice to you lately, and now you think you can talk back to me and show me attitude. I guess I'll just have to beat that attitude out of you," he says, and then his knee meets my chest.

A pained gasp escapes my lips, and I fall forward, but he grips my hair in between his fingers, keeping me upright.

"You" — slap — "must" — slap — "think" — slap — "I've" — slap — "gotten" — slap — "soft" — slap — "with" — slap — "you."

By the time he stops, my cheek is surely bruised a purplish colour, and the side of my mouth is bleeding. But he isn't done. He then lets go of my hair, and his fist immediately makes contact with my stomach, causing me to fall backwards, my back hitting the floor. He places his foot on my chest and presses down, causing me to cry out in pain.

He leans down, his hand wrapping around my throat. "The next time you disobey me, you're dead."

CHAPTER FIVE

When I wake up the next morning, my body hurts.

When I feel the hard floor beneath me, I quickly realise that I'm not in my bed. My eyes flutter open, and I notice that I'm still in the living room. I must have passed out somewhere in between getting beaten by my father.

Groaning, I get up from the floor, leaning against the wall so that I don't fall back down. My father is nowhere to be seen, and I'm grateful for that. It takes quite a while, but I manage to make it up the stairs and to my bedroom. It takes everything in me not to collapse onto my bed, especially when I see that I only have fifteen minutes to get ready. I don't even want to think about how I'm going to make it to school when my body hurts this much.

Stripping out of my clothes, I climb into the shower, letting the water fall onto me and run down my body. I'm in a terrible state with bruises littering my skin. I wash myself quickly because the hot water hurts my body, before finishing and getting dressed into my uniform. I use concealer and foundation to cover the bruises and cuts, especially the ones on my face. I can't have anyone seeing them.

By the time I'm done, I realise that school's starting in five minutes and there's no way I'll make it there in time. Sighing in frustration, I leave the house and walk to school. Luckily I'm not limping because that would have been hard to hide.

When I reach the school, I'm twenty minutes late.

"You're late," is the first thing Ms Blake says when I walk

in. However, there's an undertone of concern in her voice. She touches her hand to my arm. "Are you all right?"

She's asking me because I'm never late. I nod, smiling weakly at her before trudging to my seat.

"What's with the make-up? You never wear make-up," Lia notes when I sit down.

I merely shrug in response.

"If you wanted to try something different, you should've done the whole thing instead of just caking your face with foundation and concealer."

I smile sheepishly, turning to the front. Lia doesn't know that my father abuses me. She just thinks that my father and I don't have a good relationship. If I told her, she would force me to go and report the abuse, and even though it's the logical thing to do, I don't want to. The abuse first started when my mom passed away five years ago. I think he blames me for her death, even though I'm not sure why. It's not like cancer is something I can control. But a big part of me knows that this is his way of grieving, by placing the blame on me so that he has someone to take his anger out on. It's not a valid excuse, but in a messed-up kind of way, I understand.

It doesn't mean that I condone what he does to me, though. I remember one day he'd beaten me so badly that I had to go to the emergency room. The nurse there discretely asked me if I was being abused, but I said no, lying that I ran into a group of thugs who wanted to rob me.

The lesson goes by quickly, and in what feels like only a few minutes, the bell rings. Lia bids me goodbye and leaves for her next class while I stand up with a wince, trying not to be obvious that I'm in pain. Just as I step into the aisle, a body bumps into mine, causing me to bump my stomach into the edge of the desk. I gasp at the impact, wincing in pain.

"I'm so sorry. Are you okay?" a boy's voice asks, and I nod, not turning to look at him. He walks past me, and I hold my stomach with my hand. I'm about to move, but then I catch sight of my red-stained fingers. I look down and quickly realise that I am bleeding, blood staining my shirt just above where my skirt starts. My eyes widen in alarm.

What do I do now? I don't have anything to hide it with. Sighing, I grab my bag and rush out of the classroom, heading for the bathroom. Luckily, there's no one in the bathroom when I arrive, and I quickly run the tap, placing the bloody part of my shirt underneath the running water. I smooth it over with my fingers, trying to get rid of the stain, but instead of it disappearing, it just spreads, now becoming bigger.

Cursing under my breath, I close the tap and lift my shirt, revealing a long diagonal cut on my torso, blood seeping from the wound. I grab a paper towel and wet it before bringing it to my stomach and dabbing it onto the wound. I wince, the hotness of the water causing it to sting. I continue dabbing, but the blood won't stop flowing from the wound, dripping onto the countertop and floor.

Releasing a breath of frustration, I grab more paper towels and place them on the wound before covering it with my shirt, which I tuck back into my skirt. That will just have to work until I get home.

I use more paper towels to wipe the blood from the floor and countertop before stuffing it into the bin and walking out of the bathroom. The entire time I walk to my next class, I hold my hand onto my lower stomach, hiding the blood stain. Luckily, art class wraps up quickly, but then it's time for the class I'm dreading today . . . PE.

I merely watch as the girls slip into their sports shorts and sweaters. Lia had asked me previously why I wasn't getting dressed, and I merely told her that I wasn't feeling well and would ask the coach if I could sit this class out for today.

"You sure you're okay?" Lia asks as we leave the bathroom and head to the field.

"Yeah, I'm just running a little fever," I lie, wrapping my arms around my lower stomach. She nods, although the concern in her eyes doesn't disappear.

I walk to Coach Davis, tapping him on the shoulder to grab his attention. He turns to me, the sternness in his eyes startling me slightly. "Yes?"

"I'm not feeling so well, so I was hoping to sit this class out," I say.

He narrows his eyes at me. "What symptoms are you experiencing?"

"Uh . . . just a light fever," I answer.

"That's fine. You can just go and get a fever reducer at the nurse's office after class," he says and walks away, leaving no room for protest. Sighing, I walk back to Lia.

"And? What did he say?" she asks, and I merely shake my head. Her lips form a slight pout, and she pats me on the shoulder.

"All right, everyone!" Coach Davis yells out, blowing his whistle. "Get in a line!"

Sighing, I follow behind Lia, and we all form a diagonal line in front of Coach Davis.

"All right. So today, we'll be starting with three laps as a warm-up," he announces.

What? Three laps? I'll never make it. But just as I move to raise my hand in protest, I realise that everyone's started running already.

Coach Davis comes up to me. "Is there a specific reason why you're not running? And where's your sports attire?"

"Coach, I told you that I'm not feeling good," I say, holding my arm around my stomach.

"And I told you to go and get a fever reducer after class," he says as a matter of fact.

"Coach, I really can't—"

"Oh my gosh! Did you just get your period?" he suddenly

yells out, and my eyes immediately snap downwards. My eyes widen when I see the droplets of blood that have fallen onto the grass. From the angle that it's fallen, I can understand why he thinks that I've started my menstrual cycle, but he's a teacher and a man at that. How could he just yell it out like that?

When I look up, I notice that everyone has stopped in their tracks and are now all staring at me.

"Hey! Does anyone have a pad?" he questions, and then turns back to me shortly after. "Or do you use tampons?"

My eyes widen in horror. "What is wrong with you?"

"What's with that tone? I'm just trying to look out for you," he scolds, his eyes becoming stern.

I purse my lips as I feel everyone's gaze on me, the sight of every boy in my class staring at me, making me feel even more embarrassed.

Lia is by my side within an instant. "Are you okay? Do we need to go to the bathroom?"

I don't know what to say. All I can think about and focus on is everyone's stares on me. My breathing becomes heavy, and my heart starts racing in my chest. This is not good.

"Lia . . ." I breathe out, clutching the material of my shirt in my hand.

"Oh my, Lexi. Are you okay?" Lia exclaims, her face panic-stricken. I try to shake my head, but I fail to do so, my knees giving in.

But just as I'm about to collapse, an arm wraps around my waist and holds me up, my back hitting a hard chest. My mind feels hazy as I turn my head to look up at the person, and when my gaze meets his, my eyes widen in shock at who it is.

Rykan.

CHAPTER SIX

I can hardly believe that it's him.

Rykan. Why is he here? Is he here to help me, or is he going to embarrass me even more than I already am?

His eyes are cold as he stares down at me. Then he peels his sweater off his body, leaving him shirtless. I can't help but stare at his bare chest. He's so toned and muscular that I can hardly believe he's real. Then I see it. The tattoo of a howling wolf on the left side of his chest.

I can barely believe he's in the same class as me when he looks like this. Is he really only eighteen years old?

He pulls me out of my thoughts when he wraps the sweater around my waist, tying a knot at the front to keep it in place. And without another word, he walks away.

Lia looks speechless by what she just saw happen, but she quickly snaps out of her trance and grabs my hand. "Let's go."

She then leads me off the field and to the nurse's office. I sit down on one of the beds while Lia searches through the drawers for something. She then produces a pad from one of the drawers along with a pack of period pain tablets and brings it to me. "Take this and put the pad on in the bathroom."

I don't have the energy to tell her that the blood isn't coming from my vagina, so I just dry-swallow one pain tablet and head to the bathroom. I stand in front of the mirror, loosening the sweater's knot and unwrapping it from my body. The red stain has deepened, becoming more apparent. When I lift my shirt, I see that blood has soaked the paper towels completely with its crimson colour.

I peel the paper towels off my skin and grab clean ones, wetting them before dabbing them onto my wound. I dab it a few times before doing the same as earlier and tucking my shirt back into my skirt. I then wrap the sweater around my waist again, tying a knot so that it doesn't fall off. I stuff the pad into the bin and exit the bathroom after washing all the blood off my hands.

"You good?" Lia asks as soon as I'm out of the bathroom, and I nod. "Don't worry about what happened. It'll be a thing for a few days, but then it'll blow over, and it will be like it never even happened."

I nod, although I don't fully believe her. That was the most embarrassing thing that's ever happened to me, and I hope I never have to relive that moment.

"But I wonder why Rykan helped you. I mean, he comes off as such a cold and mean person that I'd have never imagined he'd be the one to help you even before I could," she says.

I hum in agreement. Why did he help me? I thought he hated me after I called them *dogs*. Or maybe he does. He just has a heart and pitied me.

That's probably it.

The first thing I do when I get home is grab the first-aid kit.

I disinfect the wound, wincing now and then at the stinging pain before wrapping a bandage around myself. Luckily, now that I've finally properly inspected the cut, I see that it's not so deep that I need to get stitches. Hopefully, it will heal quickly, though.

When I'm finished, I take a light shower and spend the rest of the time lying on my bed. It's only when night falls that I get up from my bed. The sandwich from last night remains untouched on the kitchen table, and I eat it as my dinner, even though it's gotten hard overnight, because I have no energy to go out and buy something.

Then I lie back down on my bed. I'm just about to fall asleep when I hear something hit my bedroom window. My eyes snap open, and I sit up, narrowing my eyes at the window. Did I imagine it? But just as that thought flutters through my mind, a stone hits my window, catching my attention. I get up from my bed and walk to the window.

Relief floods my body when I see Lia standing outside my window, waving up at me. I slide the window open.

"Is your dad home?" is the first thing she asks. I shake my head, and she runs away to the front door.

I slide the window closed and leave my room, descending the stairs before meeting Lia at the door. "What are you doing here so late?"

It's at least ten at night, the sun having gone down quite a while ago and the moon taking its place in the sky.

She holds up a flashlight. "I want us to go investigating."

Without another word, she pulls me out the door and starts leading the two of us somewhere as soon as I lock the door. It's only when the dark forest comes into view that I stop and pull her back. "What are we doing here? We're not going to . . . you know . . . go in there, right?"

She nods with a smile, but I shake my head. "You're crazy."

"Oh, come on. I have a reason. You know I won't just lead you into the darkness for fun," she says, but I'm not convinced. Just looking at the forest from a distance is scary enough, never mind actually going into it. Who knows what may linger in the darkness . . .

"No," I say, shaking my head. "There's no way I'm going in there at this hour. Why don't we just come back tomorrow when there's light?"

She shakes her head. "There will be too many eyes on us at that time. We have to do it at night."

"And why do we need to?" I question.

"Because a little birdie told me that there's secretly a mansion in the forest," she says, smiling mischievously.

"And?"

"And the residents of the mansion may or may not be werewolves," she says with a cheeky laugh.

"And you care why?" I ask, folding my arms across my chest.

She rolls her eyes at me. "Are you dense? I think it may be the transfer students."

Her words make me pause. The transfer students? Oh, now I get it. If werewolves live in the mansion and the transfer students are caught living there, that will confirm whether they're werewolves.

But although I understand why she wants to do this, I'm still hesitant. It's dangerous in there, especially if werewolves live in the centre of it. Sensing my hesitance, Lia grabs my arm and says, "Look, don't think too much. Let's just try it, and if I sense something's wrong, we'll turn back. I promise."

With a sigh, I hesitantly nod. She smiles in triumph before pulling me into the forest. Almost immediately, we're encompassed in complete darkness. Lia turns on her flashlight, and the sight of it shining onto her face makes me gasp in surprise. She merely laughs at me, finding my fear amusing. If I had half of the courage she has, I'd run for president.

Before I even realise it, we're deep into the forest, and when I turn back, I can no longer see the city lights. "Hey, don't you think we've come far enough now?"

She shakes her head. "Do you know how big this forest is? We've barely gone anywhere."

Sighing, I allow her to lead me further into the trees. Then, as if the universe hates me, the light from Lia's flashlight starts flickering.

"What's going on?" I question as she starts to hit the

flashlight with her hand. It goes off, leaving us in complete darkness.

"I must have forgotten to charge it before I left." is her sheepish answer, but I'm hardly interested in indulging her right now. Releasing a breath in frustration, I run my hand through my hair.

Then I hear something. I freeze, pulling on Lia's arm briefly.

"What?"

"Didn't you hear that?" I ask, my own voice answering me. It's only at this moment that I realise I can no longer feel Lia or her presence. "Lia? Lia, where are you?"

No matter how much I yell, all that answers me is my own voice. Panic creeps in, and my eyes dart to my surroundings. I can't see a thing, pitch blackness surrounding me. Then I see it.

Blood-red eyes, staring right at me. What is that?

"Lia?" I mutter, my voice trembling. I can't see it clearly, but judging from its eyes, it can't be anything but a monster. With one scream, I turn around and run away. I don't know how long I run, only stopping when pain erupts in my lower stomach. Toppling over, I fall to the ground in pain.

My stomach hurts, and I'm pretty sure I scratched my face from falling face-first onto the forest ground. I roll onto my side, clutching my stomach with my hand. I need to get out of here, but I'm pretty sure I just went deeper into the forest when I ran. I might have a chance if I go back where I came from, but that monster may still be there, waiting for me to return. It's a chance I'm not willing to take.

I hear a branch snapping. I freeze, my eyes wide in alert. Oh no, that monster has found me. My panic becomes more apparent, and suddenly, all I can think about is that I'm going to die here tonight. I don't want to die now. I'm still so young. There's still so much I want to do. I have dreams I want to fulfil. If I die here now, it's all over. And what about Lia? I still have no idea where she is. She could be in danger, too, or she may suffer from post-traumatic stress disorder if she stumbles across my dead body.

No, I don't want to die. I really don't want to die right now.

Closing my eyes, I mutter a string of prayers, all consisting of me asking whoever is up there to save me. Then I hear it.

"Lexia?" That voice. It sounds familiar.

My eyes snap open, and I look up. I can't see anyone. "Hello? Is there someone there?"

I really hope I didn't imagine it. This may be my way of surviving, especially since the voice called out my name, suggesting that whoever the voice belongs to knows me.

"Please. If you're hearing me right now, please help me," I plead, tears filling my eyes in desperation. When I hear the footsteps coming closer to me, I hold my breath. This is a double-edged sword. Either this person will save me, or they'll kill me. I can only hope it's not the latter.

Then, as the person comes closer, and a light appears, shining onto their face, I gasp at who I see.

Rykan.

CHAPTER SEVEN

"What are you doing out here?"

I flinch at his tone of voice. However, I can hardly care about how angry he sounds. All I can think about is that monster not too far from us and how relieved I am to see him. I don't even question what he's doing here, even though the thought that he's a werewolf who lives in the secret mansion does cross my mind, but I can save that for later. Right now, I need to put all my focus on surviving.

"Can you help me up, please?" I ask, holding my hand out to him. He sighs through his nose but doesn't say anything, just coming closer to me and kneeling. Then he does something I wasn't expecting. He sniffs the air. Oh my, is he really a werewolf?

His eyes move down, and he shines the light onto my stomach. "You're bleeding."

I gasp when I see the red stain on my top. I must have opened my wound again from all the running and from when I fell. I touch my hand to the top, and crimson red stains my fingers when I pull it away. This is a lot more blood than earlier. Turning my head to face Rykan, I ask, "What do we do?"

He releases a breath in what sounds like frustration before standing up, grabbing my hand with his and pulling me up after him. "You're bleeding from your stomach, and look at the state of your face."

I smile sheepishly, wincing in surprise when I feel pain from my open lip. I touch the cut with my finger, frowning at the blood that stains it. "It's really bad, isn't it?"

He stares incredulously at me, as if asking me if I'm being serious right now. "You should go to the hospital."

"Aren't you going to ask me where I got these wounds?" I can't help but ask. "I mean, aren't you curious? The girl in your class just appeared in front of you, bleeding."

"As long as you didn't get them out here, it's none of my business," he simply says.

"How do you know?"

"Because you came to school today with those wounds," he says.

"You knew?" I gasp.

"You didn't do a very good job at hiding it," he says, his eyebrows furrowing slightly. "Luckily for you, everyone in the school seems stupid. I mean, seriously, how could that have been your period?"

My cheeks flush in embarrassment, and I look down. "Is that why you helped me?"

He merely shrugs in response. Then he clears his throat. "If I take you back to the city, you'll be able to get to the hospital on your own, right?"

"Actually, I don't think we should return to the city," I cut in, grabbing his arm with both hands. He raises an eyebrow in questioning. "Well, you see . . . actually . . ."

"Spit it out," he says in annoyance.

"There's a monster back there," I blurt out.

He pauses. "A what?"

"A monster," I insist. "I saw it. It was staring at me with blood-red eyes. If I hadn't run away, I'm sure it would have killed me."

"I doubt it was a monster."

"I know why you think that. The thought that it was a werewolf crossed my mind, too, but I read somewhere that ghouls have red eyes, too. And that they're cannibals who eat their own kind as well as humans. What if we go back there, and it's still there? What if it tries to eat us?" I ramble.

"Then where do you suggest we go?" he asks, the facial expression on his face suggesting to me that he's already bored with this conversation. No, he can't be bored already. If he's bored, he may change his mind and leave me out here alone.

Then I get an idea. "You live here, don't you?"

His eyes flash. "Where the hell did you hear that?"

The sudden anger in his voice has me taking a step back in caution. "Nowhere. It's just a hunch."

"Just a hunch?" he questions, staring down at me in disbelief. "You really expect me to believe that?"

"Yes," I exclaim. "Otherwise, why would you be here, in the middle of the forest, so late at night?"

"What about you? What are you doing here?" His question silences me. It's not like I can tell him that I'm here hoping to catch him out as a werewolf.

"Oh, so now you're quiet?"

"Stop questioning me so much," I feebly say.

"I only asked you one question. You're the one who's been questioning me this entire time," he says.

I shrug him off. "Just take me to your place," I say, startling myself. Where did that come from? I would never say something like that.

"My place?" he questions, his eyes narrowing in suspicion.

I guess I have no choice but to go along with this. "Yes, your place," I boldly say. "It's the safest place to be right now."

"I'm not taking you to my place," he simply says.

"Then where do you suggest we go?" I ask.

"I believe I previously said that I would take you back to the city," he says, pointing behind him.

"But the monster . . ." I trail off, pouting.

"Trust me, everything will be fine," he assures. However,

the annoyance in his tone is doing nothing to convince me. "Now, shall we go before I change my mind?"

His words have me quickly nodding, not wanting to take the chance of him potentially leaving me here. He starts walking, and I quickly rush after him, grabbing onto his arm. If he minds, he doesn't say anything. Then I remember and pull him to a stop. "My friend, Lia. She came out here with me, but I lost her."

"What do you want me to do about it?" he asks in a frustrated tone.

"We can't just go back when she's still out here. She's all alone, and there's the monster that's lurking in the darkness, too," I say.

He tilts his head to the side. "I'm not going to go and look for your friend."

"But—"

"Listen here, my patience is running very low with you. If you don't come with me right now, I'm leaving you here," he threatens.

I gulp, knowing that he's not just bluffing. I'm nothing to him, so he'll definitely leave me here. But it's not like I can just leave without Lia. Who knows what may happen to her in here? "I can't leave my friend," I firmly say, shaking my head.

"And I'm not helping you find her," he firmly says, his eyes daring me to say otherwise.

"Fine," I exclaim. "I'll just find her myself then."

I turn away from him, and even though the pure darkness before me scares me, I take a deep breath and walk forward. As I walk, I mutter under my breath, "Prick."

How can he be like this? It's so dangerous in the forest, and it's nighttime, and I'm a girl. How can he just leave me be? Doesn't he feel a thing? Doesn't he have a shred of humanity?

"Wait," he suddenly says.

I halt, turning back to him with an expectant smile on my

face.

"Is there really a monster out there?"

I nod. "I told you."

Sighing, he says, "Fine. I'll help you."

A small smile tugs at my lips, but I force it down. He then holds out his hand to me. I stare down at it with furrowed eyebrows.

"Give me your hand," he says, and even though I'm suspicious as to why he suddenly wants me to hold his hand, I don't say anything, wordlessly placing my hand on top of his. Suddenly, he pulls me forward, and I crash into his chest. My eyes widen in surprise.

"Wha-what are you doing?" I stammer, my cheeks heating up.

"You need to stay close to me. If we lose each other, I'm not going to go looking for you," he says.

I nod, swallowing.

"Kiss him."

My eyes widen at the voice that resonates in my head. Why is the voice telling me to kiss him? Then, as if I've been put under a spell, my gaze flutters down to his lips, his pink plump lips. They suddenly seem so inviting. He's so close, so close that if I just pull him down by his collar, our lips will touch.

"What are you doing?" he whispers, his breath fanning my face. My eyes move up to his.

"What does it look like I'm doing?" I ask. Why am I saying this? This isn't me. He raises an eyebrow at me in suspicion, and my focus darts back to his lips, just as his tongue swipes across them, wetting them. Is he doing this on purpose?

"Do you want to kiss me?" he whispers.

I'm about to say yes, but a voice cuts in.

"Lexi?" a familiar voice calls out, snapping out of whatever trance I was in. "Lexi, are you here?"

43

I pull away from Rykan and search my surroundings to find the source of the voice. Rykan raises his light, and then I see her.

"Lia!" I gasp out, rushing into her arms. "Where did you go? Are you okay?"

"I'm okay. What about you?" she questions, her gaze scanning over my body. When she spots all my cuts and my bleeding torso, her eyes widen in alarm.

"I'm fine. I just fell, that's all," I say, hoping that she won't notice the severity of my stomach wound. She nods, causing me to release a breath of relief. Then her eyes light up, as if she has just remembered something important.

"Lexi, I failed," she whispers. "I couldn't find the mansion. No matter how much I looked, I couldn't find it."

My eyes widen at her words, and I immediately cover her mouth with my hand, preventing her from saying any more. I look at Rykan and find him staring at us with narrowed eyes.

"So that's why you were here? It wasn't just a hunch. You came here knowing about the mansion and specifically to find it."

Lia's eyes widen when she notices Rykan for the first time.

"This isn't what you think," I say, shaking my head.

"Don't you think you've lied to me enough tonight?" he questions, and even though I'm pretty sure I only told him one lie, I stay silent. "Isn't it time for you to be telling me some truth now?"

The look in Lia's eyes tells me that we're screwed, and no one knows that better than me.

"Look, we didn't come here to try anything. We were simply curious," I say. "I realise why this could make you angry, but think about it in our shoes. What would you do if you were human and unsure whether the new transfer students in your class are werewolves, and then someone tells you that there are werewolves living in the forest? Wouldn't you be curious to find out if the transfer students live there?"

"Whether or not we are werewolves, that has nothing to do with anyone. Coming here tonight is an invasion of our privacy," he says, his voice deep.

"I realise that, but —"

"No, I don't think you do because if you did, you wouldn't have come here in the first place," he says. "You came here looking for something, and guess what? You found it."

Somehow, I doubt he's talking about the mansion.

CHAPTER EIGHT

I wake up in the hospital.

The first thought that crosses my mind is — what happened?

I sit up in the bed, wincing at the slight sting in my stomach. Running my hand through my hair, I look around. I'm in a ward, but all the other beds are empty. At that moment, the door slides open, and a nurse comes walking in. Her eyes light up when they focus on me, and a warm smile appears on her face.

"You're awake," she says, coming to stand by my bedside. "How are you feeling? Any pain whatsoever?"

"There's just a little sting in my stomach, that's all," I say, and she nods. "But can you tell me what's going on? Why am I here?"

"You don't remember?" she asks, her eyebrows furrowing. I shake my head. "Well, your friend brought you here. You were passed out, so we took you in, but when I returned to speak to him, he was gone."

"Him? The person who brought me here was a male?" I question, and she nods. But I don't have any male friends. I think back to the last thing I remember. The last thing I remember is going home after school and disinfecting my wound before resting. I don't remember falling asleep, but I also don't remember anything after eating that sandwich.

Everything seems suspicious. It almost feels as though there's a big chunk missing from my memories, like it was forcefully taken from me, and that doesn't make sense.

"Did he give his name?" I ask, leaning forward slightly,

and she shakes her head.

"He was gone before I could ask," she says.

"And how long ago was that?" I ask.

"Three days ago," she answers.

"Three days ago? I was unconscious for three days?" I exclaim, and she nods.

"But luckily, during those three days, you've been healing very nicely. You don't have any facial scars, and your stitches can be taken out soon," she says, smiling down at me.

Stitches? I have stitches? I thought the cut wasn't deep enough to need stitches, but I guess I was wrong. Oh no, if I've been unconscious for three days, does that mean they've contacted my father as my guardian?

"Did you contact my father?" I ask, my eyes widening in panic when she nods. He's probably thinking that I came here on my own and that I'm planning on reporting him. This is bad. I must get out of here. No, it may be even more dangerous to leave the hospital. Who knows what he'll do to me when I arrive home? It's safer here. "When will I be discharged?"

She flips open a file, humming as she pages through it. "According to your file, you should actually be fit for discharge tomorrow."

"No." I blurt out. I can't go home so soon. I need more time. I must think of a game plan, and I need to come up with a story to tell my father.

"The doctor has already done his rounds for the day, so you'll probably only see him tomorrow. If you need anything, don't hesitate to call. There's always a nurse around," she says, flashing me one last smile before leaving the ward.

"Leave," the voice in my head suddenly says. "Leave now."

"But it's dangerous to go home," I say.

"It's even more dangerous to stay here where he can find

you," the voice says, the tone of frustration startling me slightly. This is the first time the voice has ever harboured some sort of emotion.

But the voice is right. They may call my father to let him know that I'm getting discharged since I'm still a minor. It's safer to leave now without anyone knowing. But where do I go? Then Lia comes to mind. I can stay with Lia.

Scrambling out of bed, I look around for my cell phone or clothes. I quickly find my cell phone in the cabinet drawer, but to my dismay, the battery is flat. Sighing in frustration, I take my clothes out of the cabinet and rush to the bathroom. I slip out of the hospital gown, but when I take my top into my hands, I notice the huge red stain on it. *Blood.*

If I go out wearing this, people will become suspicious. But then again, running around town in a hospital gown isn't the best idea either. People might think that I'm some crazy patient who's escaped from the hospital and report me.

Huffing in frustration, I pull the bloody top over my head and slip into my leggings and sneakers. I toss the gown into the bin before exiting the bathroom.

Now I just need to slip past the nurses without them noticing. Slowly sliding the door open, I slip out of the ward, tiptoeing down the hall. When I reach the front desk, I notice one nurse sitting in a chair there, flipping through a newspaper. I bend down onto my knees, wincing as it pulls on my cut. I then crawl across the floor to the transparent sliding doors. I freeze when the nurse coughs. Turning my head slightly, I see that she's merely shifted a little in her seat, her attention fully on the newspaper she's reading.

Releasing a breath of relief, I crawl to the sliding doors, my presence causing it to slide open, and I quickly crawl through the gap before standing up and running to the stairs. I descend the stairs, my breathing heavy by the time I reach the exit. I clutch the bloody part of my top in my hand as I rush through the entrance doors.

When I'm out of the hospital and at least a few blocks away, I finally stop to take a breather. Luckily, there's still daylight. The sun would be setting soon. It would have been dangerous for me to be out here alone if it was nighttime. I walk to Lia's house, not having any money to get a taxicab. By the time I finally reach Lia's house, the sun has already set, and darkness starts to overtake the sky.

I ring the doorbell and the door opens merely moments after. Vanessa stares at me, surprise flashing in her eyes. "Lexia, what are you doing here? Shouldn't you be in the hospital?"

"Is Lia here?" I ask, ignoring her question. Her eyebrows furrow, but she nods nonetheless and lets me in. I walk up to Lia's room, not bothering to knock before opening the door. Lia looks just as surprised as her mom to see me.

"Lexi?" she calls out, standing up from her bed and walking to me. "Shouldn't you be in the hospital?"

"Yeah, I was discharged," I lie. "But how do you know that I was in the hospital?"

"Your father called the school," she says.

He did? That's odd, to say the least. "Anyway, are you okay? How do you feel now?"

"I feel fine now. Although I could do with some clean clothes." I show her my bloody top. Her eyes widen, and she nods, rushing over to the wardrobe and pulling a random top from it before handing it to me. I thank her, pulling my bloody top over my head and slipping into her clean one.

"Don't you want to take a shower?" she asks, and I shake my head. I may have just woken up from a three-day sleep, but I'm exhausted, and all I really want to do right now is rest.

"Can I stay the night here?" I tiredly ask.

"Of course. You know you're always welcome," she says, grabbing my hand and leading me to her bed. She pulls back the covers, and I climb into bed, pulling them back over my body. "If you need anything, I'll be downstairs."

I nod, closing my eyes, and almost immediately, sleep encompasses me.

When I wake up, it's already the next morning.

I'm confused when I don't see Lia sleeping next to me as she always wakes up after me. But then I hear a knock on the door, and it opens slightly, revealing Vanessa. "Hi, you're awake."

"Yes, but where's Lia?" I ask, my eyebrows furrowing in confusion.

"She slept with me last night since you still have fresh wounds, and she didn't want to risk hurting you during the night with her wild movements," she says, and I nod in understanding. Lia's known for sleeping wildly, and that's the reason why whenever I sleep over, ninety-five per cent of the time, I wake up with her on top of me. "You can come down for breakfast when you're ready."

I nod, watching as she disappears, closing the door behind her. The first thing I need to do now is take a shower. After not washing for four days, I feel disgusting. I stand up from the bed and walk to Lia's wardrobe, pulling it open and sifting through her clothes. I pull out a loose tank top and a pair of sweatpants that I know I left here once before. I then leave the room and head to the bathroom.

Once I have stripped out of my clothes, I see that there's a bandage wrapped around my torso and that there's only a small patch of blood that's stained the bandage. I release a breath of relief. I'm not bleeding as much now, so that's a good thing. I take a quick shower, thankful when my lower stomach doesn't hurt as much as the hot water runs down my body before getting out and slipping into the clean clothes. I meet Vanessa and, surprisingly, an awake and fully dressed Lia downstairs at the kitchen table for breakfast.

"You're awake," I say to Lia in surprise. I grab the spoon and dish a little scrambled egg onto my plate, along with a sausage and tomato. She nods, looking pleased with herself as she smiles at me. I decide to play along with her. "I'm proud of you."

"It's mainly my mom's fault, but I'm happy to take the credit," she says as I softly pat her head, her leaning into my touch like a child, making me laugh. She, too, can be quite cute at times.

"What's your plan for today, Lexia?" Vanessa asks, capturing my attention. "Are you going home? I'm sure your father's worried about you."

I fight the urge to scoff at her words. Instead of worrying, I'm sure he's spending his time thinking about how to murder me. "I'm not sure."

"Well, you just came out of the hospital, so we can just relax today if you want," Lia says, and I smile gratefully at her.

"I think I'd like that, yes," I admit.

"What about your father?" her mom insists.

"I already called him. He's okay with me staying here a couple days." I lie, forcing a tight-lipped smile onto my face. Vanessa nods before getting up from her seat.

"Well, I have got to go to work. I'm not off, even on the weekend," she says with a laugh, placing her empty coffee mug into the sink. "Don't forget to clean up when you're done."

"Yes, Mom," Lia says, rolling her eyes playfully at Vanessa.

"See you girls tonight," Vanessa says before grabbing her bag and walking out of the kitchen. Almost immediately, Lia turns to me, mischief evident in her eyes.

"So, what shall we do today?" she excitedly asks, getting up and taking her plate to the sink.

"What happened to relaxing all day if I want to?" I question, raising an eyebrow at her.

"We still can. But I was thinking that maybe we could invite a few people over to relax with us," she innocently suggests, and I can't help but narrow my eyes at her in suspicion.

"What people?" I ask.

"Just people," she says with a shrug.

"Lia," I say in warning.

"Fine!" she says, jumping back onto her seat. "While you were in the hospital, I may or may not have been talking with Gage."

"Gage? As in, transfer student Gage? As in being under suspicion of being a werewolf, Gage?"

She nods.

"I thought you gave up on that."

"Nope. I gave up on Rykan, but Gage seems nice enough to turn my fantasy into a reality," she says, and I sigh, shaking my head.

"We're not inviting them over," I say, my tone leaving no room for her to protest. With a slight pout, she nods, leaning back in her seat.

Hanging out with potential werewolves? Bad idea.

CHAPTER NINE

It's time for me to go back to school.

I'm dreading it for two reasons. One . . . just relaxing at Lia's home was fun, and two . . . I'm not sure I'm ready to face reality again. Who knows, Vanessa may make me go home today, and I won't blame her if she does. I know that it's not because she doesn't want me around, but rather because she's thinking about my father. She thinks that my father's just like her, who loves, cares for, and worries about their child.

"Are you sure we don't need to go to your house to fetch your school uniform?" Lia worriedly asks, biting her lip as she stares at me. I nod, smoothing down my pants. When we woke up this morning and got ready for school, it didn't take long for me to realise that I was missing the most important thing—a school uniform.

Lia then suggested that we go and fetch it at my home, but I refused profusely. There was nothing anyone could do to make me go to that place. So from Lia's wardrobe, I just opted for plain black pants that I'm pretty sure she altered to make tighter, along with one of her school shirts, and pulled a purple cardigan on over it. I'm not sure what happens when a student breaks the dress code since I've never done it before, but I'd rather take detention and demerits than go home.

"It'll be fine," I assure her, patting her shoulder lightly. She looks more anxious than me, and I'm the one who can potentially get into trouble for this. I place my hand on my stomach as we leave the house, keeping it there the entire walk to

53

school.

Over the weekend, the cut has healed a lot, to the point that it barely hurts anymore, only giving me pain when it comes into contact with coldness, so I try to keep it covered at all times. I'm going to get my stitches taken out tomorrow, and I'm not looking forward to that. Luckily, Lia will be going with me, and I'm sure she'll have lost all feeling in her hand by the end of that appointment.

"I'm sure Ms Blake will be happy to see you. She's been so worried ever since she heard you were in the hospital," Lia says as we walk through the school gates, and I smile. I think she's the only teacher who ever worries about their students. My phone buzzes in my pocket, and I stop to answer the call, but the moment I see the caller ID, I press decline.

Lia's eyebrows furrow in confusion. "Who was that?"

"Just a telemarketer." I lie, stuffing my phone back into my pocket. It wasn't a telemarketer. In fact, it was my father. I've lost count of how many times he's called and messaged me. I briefly scanned through the messages, but they're basically just a list of curses and threats I have no doubt he'll really do if he sees me.

"Lexia!" Ms Blake exclaims when I walk into the classroom, rushing over to me and grabbing my arms. "I was so worried about you. How are you feeling now? Do you feel better?"

I nod, smiling. "I feel much better now. Thank you for worrying about me."

"Always. I see all my students as my children. I feel like, if I'm not going to worry about them, who else is going to?" she says with a smile. "Also, Lexia. If there's anything you need to talk to someone about, I'm always here."

What? Why is she telling me this?

"Don't hesitate, Lexia. Plus, I've been told that I'm a great listener and that I give out great advice countless times," she assures. "So if you're having a hard time or are in a situation that you feel you can't escape, come to me. I'll help you to the best of my ability."

"Ms Blake, do you know . . ." I trail off. No, there's no way she could know. I hide my cuts and bruises well. I've done it for so long that I'm basically a pro at it by now. There should be no reason for her to be suspicious of anything, but if she doesn't have any kind of suspicions of her own, why would she be telling me this?

She merely smiles. "Don't be afraid to ask for help, Lexia. No one can help you if you don't say anything."

She knows. I don't know how, but she knows.

And that scares me.

CHAPTER TEN

I can't stop thinking about what Ms Blake told me.

She knows. She somehow knows that I'm being abused. I don't know how she found out, nor how much of the situation she knows, but she knows something, and that's the important part. I can't believe this is happening. I thought that I hid it very well. I mean, not even Lia, who I'm very close to and sleep over at often, noticed. It just shows me how truly attentive Ms Blake is, and how much she really cares about her students.

But I don't know what to do. I'm conflicted. Do I go and tell her everything and ask for help? I feel like that's the best option for me, especially with the predicament I'm in right now, but I'm hesitant. I don't know why, but after what my own father does to me, I find it hard to trust adults. Most of them are liars who exploit children. It's something I've learnt through my own experience. If I hadn't been friends with Lia since childhood, I probably would've found it difficult to trust Vanessa, too.

Luckily, things have died down while I was in hospital. No one even recalls the incident that happened on the field, and for that, I'm grateful. The last thing I need right now is others gossiping about me.

"I'm starved," Lia grumbles as we walk to the cafeteria for lunch.

"Look, I have to go to the bathroom quickly, but you can go on ahead. I'll meet you at our table," I say.

"Are you sure? I can come with you if you want," she

offers, but I shake my head.

"I just have to change my dressing, that's all," I say, waving at her once before walking away and heading to the bathroom. The hall where the bathroom's empty. Everyone was probably having their lunch either in the cafeteria or outside right now. However, just before I reach the bathroom, I hear a voice call out my name.

Spinning around, my eyes widen when they land on the person who's called my name and who's now approaching me.

Jackson.

What does he want?

"Hi, Lexia," he says, smiling at me. I narrow my eyes at the smile he wears on his face. Why do I feel like it's not as sincere as he portrays it to be?

"Hi, Jackson. Can I help you with something?" I ask. I have every right to be suspicious. Before a couple of days ago, I had no idea that he even knew I existed, never mind knew my name. It's mainly because we've never communicated, and we basically ignore one another when passing each other at school. So why is he suddenly talking to me?

"Ouch. You hurt me, Lexia," he says with a pout. "Why do you think that I need something from you?"

"Because we've never spoken before this," I say, pointing out the obvious, and he chuckles.

"I guess that's true. But I guess there's something I want from you after all," he admits.

"And what's that?" I ask.

He smiles. "A date."

I blink in surprise. Did I hear that correctly?

"Yes, you heard me correctly. I'm asking you out on a date," he says.

"Why?" I can't help but blurt out. "We don't even know each other."

"And that's why we would go on a date. To get to know each other," he says.

All I can do is shake my head. I'm not going on a date with him. There's no way. Firstly, he's a bad boy who always gets into trouble, has probably slept with more girls than I can count on my fingers, and such a bad influence on everyone around him. And secondly, he's just not my type.

"I'm not going on a date with you," I finally say.

"And why not?" he questions.

The sudden change in his tone has me taking a cautious step back. Before, his tone was teasing, but now, suddenly, his voice has dropped a few notes, and he sounds almost . . . angry. But he has no right to be angry. It's my choice whether to say yes to a date or reject him, and I choose to reject him, and that's something he should respect.

"Because I don't want to. I don't even like you," I say, and even though it may be brutal of me to say this, it must be said.

"And? You can grow to like me as we go on dates," he protests, but I shake my head.

"I'm not interested, and I'd appreciate it if you respect that," I say with a sense of finality before turning around and walking away.

However, I don't get far before he grabs my wrist from behind and pulls me back until I crash into his chest. The harshness of his grip on my wrist has me wincing, and I immediately try to pull out of his grip, but it just gets tighter.

"Let go of me." I say out.

"You really shouldn't have rejected me, Lexi," he whispers into my ear. Then he pulls me into an empty classroom and throws me against a desk, the edge of the desk bumping into my stomach, making me wince. I turn around, holding my stomach with my hand, and he smiles, clicking the lock.

He's locked us in.

"What are you doing?" I accuse, staring at him with wide

eyes.

"You see, there are two things that I really hate in this world. The first one being werewolves, and the second being getting rejected. And you just did one," he says, his brown eyes becoming darker as he speaks.

"Listen, I don't know what you're planning on doing, but whatever it is, you need to rethink it," I warn. However, the slight tremble in my voice fails me, and he laughs at my fear, throwing his head back.

"You're so funny, you know, thinking that you have power here. It's cute, I admit," he says, a sinister smile spreading across his face.

"What do you want from me?" I question.

"What do I want from you? I want to touch you. I want to kiss you. I want to savour every inch of your body before fucking you," he says, unashamed of the words that leave his mouth. I flinch at his words. The thought of him touching me makes me shiver in disgust. There's no way he's ever laying his hands on me.

"You're sick," I say, venom laced in my voice.

"And you're mine."

Then he launches at me, pushing me back so that I fall, crashing into the desk. I land on the floor with him on top of me, and I thrash against him, clawing at him with my hands, but it's to no use when he grabs both my wrists and pins them to the ground above my head.

"Stop fighting me," he grits out. "The more you fight, the more painful it will be for you."

"I will never stop fighting," I say, glaring up at him. He merely smiles, the sinister look in his eyes setting off red flags in my mind.

"Too bad you're too weak to ever beat me," he says.

He leans down, and when his lips near mine, I turn my head. He doesn't like this because he then alternates holding my wrists down with his one hand and uses the other to grip my face harshly and force it to face his again. The only thing I can do is glare at him.

"Don't glare at me," he warns, but I don't stop.

And when he leans down again, I lift my knee and hit him in the genitalia with it. He gasps in surprise, and I use that opportunity to push him off me. He falls back with groan, clutching himself.

I scramble to my feet and run to the door, but just as my fingers touch the lock, he's grabbing my hair from behind, pulling me back. He forces me to my knees and drags me across the floor before lifting me up and throwing me against the window. I hear a crack as my head hits the glass, and then his hand is around my throat, holding me in place.

"Please. Just stop this," I plead, but he merely laughs.

"It's your own fault. You should've just obeyed me in the first place. But you had to defy me, and now this is your punishment." He chuckles, staring at me like a madman. He leans down again, but this time, he inches closer to my neck, and then he pauses.

"What's this?" He growls, and I flinch, noticing how he stares at my neck. He saw my tattoo. "Why the hell do you have a tattoo of a wolf?"

He growls at me like an animal, as if I've just personally harmed or insulted him. It's just a tattoo, and it's mine. Why does he care?

"Because I wanted it! Why? What does that have to do with you?" I yell out.

"You know how much I hate werewolves," he says, his voice deadly. His grip on my throat tightens, and my breath hitches. Is he going to kill me? "You've been a naughty girl, Lexia. And it's time for your punishment."

Then I see it. I can hardly believe what I'm seeing. His eyes, they're glowing, a bright yellow colour. I gasp in realisation.

He's a werewolf.
Then his fangs pierce my skin.

CHAPTER ELEVEN

I wake up with a gasp.

My eyes immediately dart to my surroundings, and I quickly realise that I'm in the nurse's office. I release a breath of relief, but my relief is short-lived when images of what happened before I passed out flash in my mind, and my eyes widen.

Jackson. He's a werewolf. And he bit me.

I scramble off the bed and rush to the bathroom. I bare my neck to the mirror, gasping when I see it. A bite mark, deep into my flesh and stained with dry blood. Oh no, what does this mean? Why would he bite me? What was he trying to achieve?

I touch my fingers to the bite, wincing afterwards. It hurts.

What do I do now? Do I tell the nurse a werewolf bit me and have her give me something for the pain? No, I feel like I shouldn't do that. Should I tell Lia? Or should I tell the transfer students? If they're werewolves, they should be able to know what to do to fix this. But what if they aren't actually werewolves? What if they're actually human?

What should I do?

Then I spot something else. Large purplish-blueish handprints on my throat.

Jackson must have bruised me when he put his hands around my throat.

I groan, gripping my hair with my fingers and tugging at the roots. Why must this happen to me? What did I do to deserve this? I just came out of the hospital after getting beaten.

I'm hiding from my abusive father, and now this? When do I get a break?

"Lexi?" I hear a familiar voice call out through the door. My eyes widen, and I immediately pull my hair out of its ponytail, using my hair to cover the bite mark. I wrap the hair tie around my wrist, taking a deep breath before leaving the bathroom.

Lia's eyes widen when she sees me, and she rushes over. "Are you okay? When you didn't return for lunch, I got worried."

"How long was I missing?" I ask.

"Missing?" she asks, her eyebrows furrowing in confusion, and I curse under my breath at my poor choice of words. "It hasn't been that long. Although, this is the first class I could get a bathroom break since lunch."

"And what period is it?" I slowly ask.

"Last period," she answers.

So it's been at least three hours that I must have been lying there, unconscious. "Were you here the entire time?"

"Yeah," I lie. "I was feeling a little under the weather, so I came to lie down for a while. Sorry I didn't let you know."

"It's fine, but what's wrong? Is it your cut or something?" she worriedly asks, but I shake my head.

"I'm fine, don't worry," I assure her. "Let's get to class."

We walk to our last class of the day, which so happens to be given by the one teacher in this school who hates everyone, or at least that's what it appears to be. Ms Mathews. She's extremely strict and gives detention for every little thing. I've managed to remain on her good side all year, but suddenly, as we near her class, I'm acutely reminded of my attire. Luckily for me, no teacher has said anything that or lack of a book throughout class, but I just know Ms Mathews will be the one to say something.

"Miss Leigh. What are you wearing?" she says first thing

when I enter the classroom. Her eyes are already judging me before I even have a chance to say anything.

"I had a little accident this morning, so I couldn't put on my uniform," I lie.

She narrows her eyes at me, adjusting her glasses. Ms Mathews looks like the cliché strict teachers in books, with her famous pencil skirt and school-style shirt, her pointed shoes, and her hair always pinned up in a neat bun with her thick-rimmed glasses perched on her nose. She also has a big mole underneath her left nostril.

"And where's your bag?" she asks.

"I also couldn't bring my bag today," I say with a sheepish smile.

Then her eyes move to my neck. "Please, if you're into rough acts in the bedroom, we do not need to know it."

My hand flies to my neck, and everyone snickers. I again use my hair to cover the bruises. However, I'm certain that at some point, it'll be visible to the eye again.

"It's . . . it's not like that." I say, stammering, but she stops me by raising her hand into the air.

"Just sit down, but I will warn you. Show up to my class like this again, and you'll receive detention," she warns, and I nod, swallowing uncomfortably.

I rush to my seat, my cheeks heating up in response to the outright embarrassment Ms Mathews caused. But just as I'm about to sit down, I feel a stare on me, and I raise my gaze. My heart stops when my eyes meet Rykan's.

Why's he staring at me?

We stare at one another for a few long moments before he looks away. My eyebrows furrow in confusion, but I word-lessly sit down, shrinking into my seat. I borrow a piece of paper from Lia to make notes on. However, I can barely focus on what's being said because throughout the entire lesson, I feel a hard stare at the back of my head. I want to turn around to see who's staring at me the whole time, but I hesitate, and

I'm not sure why, though.

No, I do know why. What Jackson did to me has scarred me, and even though he's not here with me, I still feel anxious. He can be watching me from afar. I mean, who knows how long he's been keeping his eye on me? I wouldn't even be surprised if he stalked me.

But there's another thought that nags at my mind. Being the curious person that I am, I did some reading on werewolves because I want to know about them, especially since they live among us. In most of the books I read, they spoke about mates. The concept was a little foreign to me, so I did more research into it. According to what I found, a mate is a werewolf's other half, their soulmate. It's the person their god paired them up with, and werewolves can only have werewolf mates. There's no such thing as a werewolf being mated to a human.

And this is what confuses me because Jackson bit me, and from what I've read, when a werewolf bites someone, it's usually to claim them, but this doesn't make sense. Doesn't Jackson have a mate of his own? If so, why did he bite me?

Does his mate even know what he's done?

The bell ringing pulls me out of my thoughts, and I quickly stand up, brushing off my thoughts. However, just as I step into the aisle, just like once before, I bump into someone. And just like before, it's Rykan.

"Don't say anything," I say, holding my hand up in the air. I vividly remember how he scolded me the first time I bumped into him, and I really don't need a repeat of that. Without another word, I brush past him and walk out of the classroom. I don't even realise that I didn't even say goodbye to Lia before leaving until I've completely left the school grounds, too consumed by my own thoughts.

Then, as if by instinct, I'm standing in front of my home. I sigh in frustration. I was so lost in my thoughts that I didn't even pay attention to where I was going. My body acted on reflex, bringing me back to the place that I've spent the last few days avoiding.

I should turn around and go to Lia's house. I should, but even as my brain yells at me to get away from here, I stay rooted in my spot. I suppose it won't hurt to just go in briefly and grab a few of my things for my stay at Lia's home. It should be safe because my father's rarely home at this hour anyway.

Yes, it should be fine.

I recite those words like a mantra in my head as I enter the house. It's quiet, luckily. I run up the stairs and to my room, grabbing my schoolbag that's on my bed before grabbing random items of clothing from my wardrobe along with my school uniform and stuffing them into a separate duffle bag I find underneath my bed. After zipping the bags closed, I throw them over my shoulders and walk out of my room. However, just as I reach the top of the staircase, the front door opens, and someone comes walking in. My eyes widen in panic at who I see.

My father.

CHAPTER TWELVE

M y father isn't alone.

After him, three other men his age come walking in, and I immediately recognise them. They are my father's friends. The same friends who frequently ask my father to make me *entertain* them.

I rush back into my room, closing the door behind me. I have to get out of here, now. My eyes find the window, and I know. The only way for me to get out of here right now is through my window. But as I slide the window open and look down, I hesitate. It's a two-storey jump down, and I've never done it before. I can really end up hurting myself.

But then again, that's nothing compared to what my father will do to me should he find me here. I have to do this. This is the only way. So I take a deep breath, clutching the straps of my bags before leaping forward.

The fall is quick, and I hit the ground feet first. However, I quickly stumble from the impact and topple over, falling face-first onto the ground. I groan, rolling onto my side. My legs hurt, and it's a miracle I didn't break both of them. I barely manage to get to my feet when I hear the front door open, and I freeze. My landing must have alerted them, and they've come out to check what it is.

When my eyes meet my father's, fear creeps in. A sinister smile appears on his face, and without wasting another second, I dash out into the open street before jumping onto the sidewalk and running. I can hear yelling from behind me, but I don't pay any attention to it, focusing on getting away from my father.

When I turn my head around briefly, I see my father and his friends running after me, anger evident on their faces. Then when I turn my head, I crash into something hard. A pair of strong arms catch me before I fall, pulling me up against their chest. My eyes meet a pair of chocolate-brown ones, and I'm surprised when I see those familiar golden specks.

Rykan.

His eyebrows furrow at my panicked state, but before I can even say anything or run away, I hear my father calling out my name. I turn around in Rykan's arms, my eyes filled with fear. My breath hitches when my father and his friends stop merely a few metres away from Rykan and me. I'm in trouble. Even if I try to run now, I'll never be able to get away. I'm done for.

"Lexia, come here," my father says, gesturing me to come to him with his hand, and my immediate reaction is to move back, pressing my back against Rykan's chest.

"Lexia, come here while I'm still being nice."

"What's going on here?" Rykan asks from behind me, his voice startling me slightly.

"Boy, just mind your own business. This is between me and my daughter," my father says.

"Yeah. Get lost, boy," one of my father's friends chimes in.

A few moments of silence pass by, and then I feel Rykan moving.

Almost immediately, I speak, "Don't go."

His entire body tenses against me as he freezes.

"Please. Don't go," I softly plead, hoping that he'll listen. If there's anything I've noticed about him, it's that he doesn't care about anyone besides the other two transfer students, but even though I doubt he'll stay and help me, I have to try. Then Rykan spins me around in his arms, his eyes finding my exposed neck.

"Did he do this to you?" he questions, his tone deadly. I want to say no, but instead, I nod. Who knows? Maybe if I tell the truth, he'll just leave. Something flashes in his eyes, and they narrow slightly at my form. For a split second, it looks as though he knows that I'm lying, but once his eyes land on my shaky hands and trembling lips, it vanishes. Then his eyes are back on my father and his friends. "What do you want with her?"

"Boy, didn't I tell you to butt out?" my father says, his eyes darkening.

My hand instinctively grabs Rykan's arm, my fingers trembling from fear. Rykan quickly notices, and he pulls me closer, his hand going to my hip and staying there. Even in this situation, I can't help but notice how surprisingly attentive he is.

"And didn't I ask you what you want with her?" Rykan says, nodding to me with his head.

"It's none of your business what I want with my daughter," my father says nastily.

"It is when she's running from you, scared for her life," Rykan says back. He's not backing down, but neither is my father.

"Look, I don't know who you are, but you have no right to interfere here. Now leave before I do something you'll regret," my father says, threateningly.

Rykan merely smiles. "I think it's the other way around, though."

My father scoffs. "And what makes you so confident, boy?"

My father places emphasis on the word boy as if to exert his dominance, since he's a man and Rykan's merely a teenager.

"What makes you so confident, old man?" Rykan asks.

Rykan is ticking my father off, I can tell. We can both tell, and I think that Rykan's doing it on purpose.

"Wow," my father says to his friends. "He really doesn't know who he's dealing with, huh?"

His friends laugh, taunting Rykan with their stares. Rykan, however, doesn't even flinch, staring blankly at them.

"Boy, I'll give you one last chance. Leave," my father warns. "Trust me. She's not worth the trouble."

My heart clenches at his words. Is he right?

Rykan's hand on my hip twitches, and his grip tightens.

"And who are you to decide that?" he slowly asks. His voice, there's something in his voice that's changed, and I'm not the only one who's noticed. My father's eyes widen slightly, and I may be wrong, but I see fear flash in them. His friends take a step back in caution. "Who gave you the right?"

His voice. Why does it sound like two people are talking? My head lifts, and my eyes widen when they see his. His eyes . . . they've changed.

They're glowing.

CHAPTER THIRTEEN

R ykan is a werewolf.
And now my father knows.

His eyes . . . they're glowing a vibrant molten gold colour. It's the exact same colour as the usual golden specks that surround his pupil.

"You're . . . you're a were—werewolf," my father says, stammering. His eyes widen as he points his finger at Rykan.

"Rykan," I whisper to him, and his grip on my hip tightens in response. I don't know what's happening to him, but whatever it is, it needs to stop. The last thing we need is innocent people passing by, seeing his glowing eyes and shouting werewolf. "Rykan, look at me."

He doesn't budge, glaring at my father with those glowing eyes of his. Unable to stop myself, I grasp his face in between my hands and pull it down to mine.

"Rykan," I whisper, capturing his attention. His golden eyes flutter to mine, and their brilliance strikes me frozen for a moment before I break out of it. Now is not the time to appreciate his beautiful eyes. "Rykan, it's okay. Calm down."

His eyebrows furrow slightly, almost as if he's having an internal battle with himself. Finally, slowly but surely, the golden colour fades, leaving behind his normal brown orbs. I nod at him as he returns to me.

"You're okay," I whisper, smiling softly at him. He stares down at me, confusion swirling in his irises.

"Who are you?" he whispers in disbelief. His words confuse me, but before I can ask him what he means, my father's

71

voice cuts in.

"Werewolf!" he yells out, and my eyes widen in panic. "He's a werewolf!"

"Shut up," I yell.

"You . . . what are you doing with a werewolf?" my father questions, pointing his finger at Rykan.

"Don't point your finger at him," I say, feeling weirdly protective over Rykan. The suddenness of it confuses me, but now is not the time to dwell on that. "And what I do with him is none of your business."

My father scoffs. "Wow. My own daughter is busy with a werewolf. I should've expected it."

"Shut up," Rykan says from behind me, seeming to break out of whatever trance he was in.

"Just leave, Father," I say with a sigh. He glares at me. "Unless you want to die."

Will Rykan kill him? I'm not sure, but either way, if my father believes that he will, it should be enough to get him to leave. At least for now.

My father hesitates, once, twice, before turning to his friends and gesturing them to leave with him. He spares me one last glance before walking away, his three friends trailing closely behind him, although I don't fail to notice the look one of them sends my way, the way his eyes scan over my body, and he licks his lips after, making me uncomfortable.

I follow them with my eyes, only looking away once they disappear around the corner. I release a breath, relief flooding my body. "Oh, thank God."

Only when I become acutely aware of Rykan's remaining hand on my hip can I bring my attention back to him. I find him already staring down at me, a certain confusion in his eyes startling me. Also, there's something else there, too. I could be mistaken, but his eyes seem almost . . . soft.

"Are you okay?" I softly ask.

"Shouldn't I be the one asking you that?" he questions, the previous look in his eyes disappearing as he speaks.

"Well . . . I guess that's debatable," I say with a light laugh. It's a miracle that I can still laugh after what just happened.

"Are you?" he asks, the gentleness in his voice surprising me. "Okay, I mean."

"As okay as I can be considering what just happened, I guess," I answer.

"What did just happen?" he asks.

I don't answer. I'm not sure I'm ready to tell anyone my story, especially someone who was so cold to me before. This sudden change in him may even be temporary because he pities me, and when tomorrow comes, it'll be gone.

"You don't have to tell me if you don't want to. I don't want to invade your privacy or anything."

Invade my privacy . . . why does that sound so familiar, as if he's said it to me once before? I shrug off the thought, regarding it as nothing.

"Thank you," I say instead of voicing my thoughts. "And thank you for helping me. I don't know what I would've done if you didn't help me."

He doesn't respond, merely staring at me.

"Why are you staring at me like that? It's not the first time," I say. In the span of these few minutes, he's stared at me in a certain way, a way that I don't understand. "Is something perhaps wrong?"

"No, nothing's wrong. I'm just . . . confused," he says, and I blink in surprise.

"Confused?" I ask with furrowed eyebrows.

"This . . . you . . . it's all so strange," he says, blinking at me in confusion.

Strange? What does he mean by that?

Then I realise. There's a big elephant that we've yet to address.

"So . . . you're a werewolf," I find myself saying, cringing at my tone of voice. I didn't mean to, but I came out sounding quite awkward, to say the least.

Rykan flinches at my words, realisation flashing in his eyes. He doesn't respond immediately, appearing to be thinking about what to say.

I know why he's unsure of what to say. I just found out possibly his deepest secret, and he doesn't want to say something that may trigger me into telling everyone.

But just as he appears to want to say something, a pounding sensation erupts throughout my neck. I flinch, my eyes widening.

"What . . . what's wrong?" he asks, looking alarmed as he stares at me.

I suppose now is the best time to show him what's happened to me. With shaky fingers, I pull my hair out of the way, baring my neck to him. He looks confused as to what I'm doing at first, but when his eyes land on the raw bite mark on my neck, his eyes widen.

"What the hell is this?"

I flinch when his fingers touch the bite, moving to the back slightly. It hurts when touched.

"Who the hell did this to you?" he demands, anger seeping into his voice.

"That's not important right now. What's important is that . . ." I trail off as my vision becomes blurry and everything quietens. My legs start to feel weak, and barely a moment later, I fall.

Rykan catches me in his arms, placing his hand on my cheek. "Hey, stay with me. Stay with me, damn it."

He sounds panicky, but all I can do is stare up at him with dazed eyes, unable to say a word. And soon, I start to feel my eyes going closed. His widen.

"No, don't fall asleep," he rushes out, patting my cheek

with his hand. "Stay with me."
And darkness consumes me.

CHAPTER FOURTEEN

Everything is dark.

I can feel the presence of people, their auras all hovering over me. They're speaking in hushed tones, as if they're afraid I can hear them. I can't understand most of what they're saying, but one statement stands out to me.

"She's going to die."

I'm going to die? Panic creeps into me, but I can't move. *I'm stuck.*

"We have to save her," one voice says.

"But how? There's only one way I can think of, but it's dangerous," another says.

"Cole's right. It could have serious consequences."

"Rykan, what do you think?"

"Yes, you're the one who's going to have to deal with it. Whatever you say, we'll go with it."

Silence follows.

Please. Say something. Anything. I don't want to die.

"Let's do it."

Do what? What are they going to do to me?

Then I feel it. Warm breath on my face. He's so close to me. *Wait, he? Who is he? What am I thinking?*

I'm about to die.

Then I feel something wet on my neck, the feeling of it swiping across the bite causing me to wince. Then I feel it. Teeth — no, fangs — piercing my skin.

I scream, pain flooding my body. But it vanishes within an instant, a warm sensation washing over me and wrapping itself around my heart.

A scent instantly invades my nostrils. It's nice, smelling like cinnamon and vanilla, with a hint of nature, the forest.

"It's done," a voice announces.

"Now we wait."

And darkness envelops me again.

CHAPTER FIFTEEN

Everything is silent.

My eyes flutter open, blinking as they focus. The first thing I see is a white ceiling. At first I'm unable to move, my limbs rooted in place. It takes me a few minutes to finally be able to move my pinkie finger, and the rest of me follows easily.

I'm in a room, all alone. I'm lying in a soft bed, my head pushed back into plush pillows. I slowly sit up, and the duvet slips off my body as I do.

The only emotion apparent in me is confusion. Where am I?

This room doesn't strike me as familiar at all. It's a big room, with floor-to-ceiling sliding doors opposite the bed, revealing a balcony with a view of the forest. There are two doors on the other end, one against the wall, which I'm assuming leads to a bathroom, and the other out of the room. I get up from the bed and walk over to the sliding doors. I slide open one of the doors and step out onto the balcony.

I'm standing on the balcony of a two-storey house that overlooks the trees and even the lake nearby.

I hear a door open, capturing my attention. I turn around in my spot, staring into the room. Then a familiar scent fills my nostrils. Cinnamon and vanilla. I'm not sure why, but I have an overwhelming urge to run to the source of the scent and wrap my arms around it, if it even belongs to a person.

But I resist the urge, remaining rooted in my spot.

"Lexia?" I hear a familiar voice call out. Rykan.

A warm feeling swells up in my chest, and I unknowingly

smile. Why, though, I'm unsure. The sudden rush of foreign emotions scares me a little. So I step aside, hiding at the edge of the balcony so that he can't see me out here.

Then another person walks in. "Where is she?"

There's immediate panic in the person's voice, but I don't hear Rykan respond. Footsteps follow the silence, and before I even realise it, Rykan steps through the sliding door I left open. His head snaps to the side, his eyes meeting mine.

Mine widen as a strange feeling washes over me. I feel warm, and unbidden, my cheeks flush with heat under his stare. I look away, redness burning my cheeks as my heart races at an abnormal speed in my chest.

What's going on with me?

Am I sick? Because this isn't a natural reaction. I barely know the man, yet my heart races, and I blush upon seeing him.

"You're awake," he says, pulling me out of my thoughts. He comes closer to me. "Are you okay? How are you feeling?"

How am I feeling? Confused and overwhelmed. I feel like a lot's happened, and there's a lot I don't know. I also feel like he has all the answers to my questions, yet he avoids mentioning them even though I'm sure he can imagine what must be going on in my head right now.

"Lexia," he suddenly calls out, grabbing my attention.

"Huh?" I distractedly mutter, my eyes snapping up to his.

"Is something the matter?" he asks, but I don't answer. "What's wrong? Are you feeling ill? Are you in any pain?"

When his hand touches my forehead, the heat in my cheeks becomes more apparent, and I wish that he wasn't so close to me right now so that I could hide my blush from him. He looks down, his eyes meeting mine. Our stare has my blush deepening to the point that it feels as though my face is on fire, and there's no doubt that he can see it. His eyebrows furrow, and then his eyes soften.

I want to hug him.

This sudden desire startles me, and it's only my slight fear that stops me from leaping into his arms and letting him hold me.

Then a familiar head pops out through the opening. Gage. His eyes widen upon seeing me.

"You're awake," he gasps, breaking Rykan's and my moment. "How are you feeling? Are you in any pain?"

What's with them asking me that? Why would I be in pain?

Then my last memories come flooding into my mind—Jackson, the bite, my father, another bite, and passing out. My hand flies to my neck, the action catching both of their eyes. I trail my fingers across the scarred and newly healed skin, biting my lower lip as I make the shape of the scarred skin out as a bite mark.

Dread fills me. Jackson's mark is still on me.

Unable to stop myself, I step forward, pressing my cheek against Rykan's chest and wrapping my arms around his waist. He tenses underneath my touch, but it doesn't bother me, but tears fill my eyes. I sniffle, and that grabs his attention.

"Are you . . . are you crying?" he hesitantly asks, an undertone of nervousness in his voice.

I nod, snuggling my face against his chest. Tears fall from my eyes, rolling down my cheeks, and my body shakes.

Slowly and very hesitantly, his arms come around me, and he embraces me back.

This feels nice. His arms around me, his warmth, and his scent engulfing me. I don't know how long we stand here before I shiver, the breeze becoming cold. Rykan quickly notices, rubbing his hands up and down my arms. "Are you cold?"

I nod against his chest, another sniffle escaping me.

"We should go inside then," he says, but I shake my head, tightening my arms around him. He sighs, and before I even realise that he's moving, his arms are under me, one underneath my thighs and the other on my lower back, and he's lifting me up bridal style. I instantly wrap my arms around his neck, snuggling my face into his neck as he holds me and carries me back into the bedroom, briefly letting go of me to slide the door closed with his one hand before he returns it to my back.

He carries me to the bed, placing me gently onto the covers, but when he pulls away from me, I catch his wrist with my hand, staring up at him with teary eyes.

He seems to understand because he quickly sits down opposite me and says, "It's okay. I'm not going anywhere."

I nod, pouting slightly. I'm not sure when Gage left, but I'm glad that he did.

"Now," Rykan starts, capturing my attention. "You need to tell me everything that happened."

"About what?" I ask, tilting my head in confusion.

"The bite. How did you get it? Who gave it to you?"

I freeze, my body tensing. How I got bitten . . . that was a traumatising ordeal that I wish I never have to talk about, but I guess it's best that I tell him, especially since he too is a werewolf.

"It was Jackson," I start, looking down at the bedsheets. "He cornered me on my way to the bathroom and suddenly confessed his feelings for me. He asked me out, but I rejected him because I hardly know him and don't like him. But then he grabbed me and threw me into an empty classroom and locked the two of us in. He hurt me, grabbed me by my hair and dragged me across the floor. He even tried to forcefully kiss me. I fought back, but he was too strong. He threw me against a window, and that's when he . . ."

I can't bring myself to say the words, flinching as I think about it. I notice how Rykan's hands twitch at his sides, as if he wants to touch me and comfort me but isn't sure if he should do it or not.

"That bastard," he says, cursing, anger seeping into his

voice. "Jackson . . . he's the one that attacked me and my friends in the cafeteria, right? He called us monsters, yet he's one of us. The audacity."

"But, Rykan, what do we do now? I read that werewolves bite someone to claim them. His mark is on me," I say, my lips trembling as I speak. The mere thought of Jackson having a claim over me disgusts me.

"Don't worry about that. The bite on your neck isn't his," he assures me, but he leaves me so confused. If it isn't Jackson's, then whose is it?

"Whose bite is it then?" I ask, and I don't fail to notice how his entire body tenses at my question. He hesitates for a long while, before finally, he answers, "It's mine."

CHAPTER SIXTEEN

It's his bite?

Did I hear him correctly? How can it be his? Then I recall the dazed memory I have. A memory of him talking with other people before he bit me.

Oh my. Rykan bit me. Does this mean that he now has a claim on me? My eyes widen in realisation, and instinctively, I stare up at Rykan with accusatory eyes. His eyes widen at my glare, his hands lifting into the air in defence. "Woah. What's up now?"

"You're not any better than Jackson. That's what's up," I say, pursing my lips in anger.

He looks like I just attacked him. "What the hell is that supposed to mean?" he asks, his eyes wide.

"You bit me just like Jackson did. Did you think that I would feel better if it's your bite on me instead of his?" I say, glaring at him.

"Okay, firstly, don't compare me to that person ever again. And secondly, do you think I wanted to bite you?" he says in anger, causing me to flinch. "Having you bear my mark was the last thing I wanted, but I had to do it to save you."

"What do you mean?" I ask, my voice softening.

He sighs through his nose, running his hand through his hair, ruffling it with his fingers, causing it to fall messily onto his forehead. I hate the way I notice.

"I'll try to explain this in simple terms so that you can understand," he starts off.

I roll my eyes at his words. I'm not stupid. I've done my

fair share of research on werewolves, so I'm not completely new to the subject.

"When a werewolf bites a human, they die, and that's why we don't do that or not supposed to do that. I'm a part of a rare breed of werewolves who have abilities special to regular werewolves, and one of those abilities is what I used to save you."

He pauses to take a breather, and I lean forward slightly, staring intently at him.

"There's a kind of ritual we can complete to save a human, but it's hardly ever used because, generally, werewolves don't claim anyone but their mate. Anyway, a pure-blood, what I'm called, bites the human, fusing the two of them together.

His last words confuse me. "I'm sorry, what?" I mutter, furrowing my eyebrows in confusion.

"I basically forged a bond between the two of us," he says, and I nod. "So that bond will give you new abilities."

"New abilities?" I can't help but cut in, thinking out loud.

"Yes, new abilities, abilities like that of a werewolf. You won't be able to shift, but you'll have abilities such as heightened strength, better hearing, speed, healing, etcetera," he explains.

My hand immediately moves to my lower stomach, and I lift my shirt up, revealing a faded long diagonal scar, but it's completely healed. *Is this because of his bite?*

I look up at him, and as if he can hear my question, he nods.

"So . . . I'll be like a werewolf but not really a werewolf?" I slowly ask.

He nods.

"I'm sorry. This is just all so confusing."

"It's okay. I expected it to be," he says, although the forced smile on his face does nothing to calm my nerves. "Anyway, back to our bond. It's almost like a mate bond, except there are a few disadvantages for you."

"What kind of disadvantages?"

"For starters, only you will feel the effects of the bond. I won't feel anything," he starts, hesitating slightly. "You will fall in love with me."

"I'm sorry, what?" I blurt out, unsure if I heard him correctly.

"As a consequence of the bond, you'll fall in love with me just like two newly bonded mates fall in love, but because you're not my mate, I won't feel anything for you," he says with a wince, as if he pities me. "You'll seek comfort in me at difficult times and —"

"I think I already feel the effects of the bond," I say, cutting him off. "Ever since I woke up, all I've been wanting to do is be around you and be in your arms."

I can't help but cringe at my own words. We met merely a week ago, and here I am, practically confessing my feelings to him. What has my life come to?

Rykan looks beyond uncomfortable as he listens to me talk, rubbing the back of his neck with his hand. He looks speechless, and he avoids my eyes, staring down at the bedsheets.

"Please say something," I practically beg because his silence is making me anxious.

He opens his mouth, but then closes it again. Then again. He looks truly speechless. Right now, I wish I had the ability to read people's minds because I'd really like to know what's going on in his mind. Although, judging by how uncomfortable he looks, I doubt I truly want to know.

Suddenly, the urge to leave this place creeps in and overwhelms me. And I feel like I should listen to it. I have no idea where I am, but one thing I'm certain of is that I don't belong here. I need to leave.

Without saying a word to Rykan, I move over to the edge of the bed, but just as I'm about to get up, his hand wraps around my wrist, stopping me. "Where are you going?"

Oh, so now he has something to say.

"I'm leaving," I announce. Saying those two words hurt me, and my heart clenching in a way that can only be from the bond.

"Why?" he asks, his eyebrows furrowing.

"Isn't it obvious? I don't belong here. You've made it clear that you want nothing to do with what's happened, so I don't see any reason to stay," I say.

"Look, don't misunderstand me—"

"No, I don't think it is possible to misunderstand you when you've made yourself very clear," I say, pulling my wrist out of his hold. I get off the bed and slip into a pair of slippers I didn't even notice were here until now. A part of me expects Rykan to stop me, but when my hand wraps around the door handle and I pull the door open, I realise that he's not going to.

What did I even expect? Like he said before, this bond won't affect him.

I'm the only one falling in love.

CHAPTER SEVENTEEN

*M**y heart aches.*

As I descend the staircase, my heart clenches uncomfortably in my chest. Is this what heartbreak feels like?

The further I get from Rykan's room, the more my heart pains. Why do I have to feel this way? Tears fill my eyes, but I quickly wipe them away before they can fall. I feel so helpless. I'm alive, and I guess I should be grateful for that, but it's at the price of my heart.

My heart now no longer belongs to me. It's now not my own, and I hate that. I want to be able to fall in love the natural and traditional way. I want to meet someone, get to know them, and fall in love with them as time passes. But that's just wishful thinking because now Rykan has stolen my heart, and I'm not sure I can trust him with it.

I don't pay attention to my surroundings as I exit the house, my slipper-clad feet touching the leaves as I step off the porch. It's only when I finally look around that I notice where I am, although it's foreign to me. This house is situated on a huge plot of land in the forest, surrounded by smaller houses and cottages.

How do they manage to hide such a big place from the rest of the world? It looks like a village all its own.

I sigh, realising that I'll get lost trying to leave this place, but my pride won't let me turn around and go back to Rykan. Instead, I walk on, trying to ignore the slight anxiousness that creeps in. Before I even realise it, I reach a group of people— no, a group of werewolves. They all watch as two other werewolves circle one another, preparing to fight. What's happening?

Suddenly, all their heads snap to me as they realise my presence. I freeze, my heart stopping. They all stare at me with narrowed eyes, and I gulp in fear. What are they going to do to me now?

"Who the hell are you?" a girl with long blonde hair and crystal blue eyes says. "You're human."

They all gasp at her words, and my eyes widen in panic.

"What the hell are you doing here human?"

I flinch at the tone of a male voice, pursing my lips as he bares his teeth at me. And when he takes a step forward, I take one back. I flinch when I step onto a branch, snapping it beneath my feet.

"You've made a grave mistake, human," he says, his voice low and threatening.

"Please don't hurt me," I plead, my voice soft and vulnerable. They all burst out laughing, finding my fear very amusing.

"You're dead," he says, but just as he prepares to pounce on me, a vicious growl erupts through the area, causing him to flinch, and as if by instinct, he stops and bows his head. My eyebrows furrow in confusion, but when an arm wraps around my shoulder, and the familiar vanilla and cinnamon fills my nostrils, I realise who it is.

"What the hell do you think you are doing?" Rykan growls.

"Alpha, this human has invaded our territory. I was merely trying to get rid of her," he answers, not lifting his head.

Alpha?

"And you didn't think to report to me about this first?" Rykan questions.

"I didn't want to bother you with something this trivial, Alpha," he answers, a tremble evident in his voice.

"Trivial? That's for me to decide," Rykan says, his voice powerful and dominant.

"I apologise, Alpha. It wasn't my intention to anger you."
Then a gust of wind rushes by, causing my hair to fall back.
Someone gasps in horror, pointing their finger at me. Everyone's eyes follow where she's pointing to, and I quickly realise where they're all looking.

My neck.

My eyes widen. The bite mark.

"It's . . . it's the Alpha's mark," a middle-aged lady stammers out, and gasps erupt throughout the werewolves. The
eye of the man who threatened to kill me widen, and he immediately drops to his knees.

"Alpha, I'm so sorry. I had no idea who she is to you. I deserve to die," he rushes out, his voice panicked.

Die? Isn't that too extreme?

My head lifts, and I look up at Rykan, my eyes widening
when he doesn't disagree with the man, but instead appears
to be considering it as he glares down at the man.

"Rykan," I call out softly, but it grabs his attention, his glare
ceasing and his head turning to mine. "That's enough."

I'm not even sure what I'm doing or if it'll even sway
Rykan a little, but I feel like I have to try. It's strange, though.
Why do I suddenly feel the need to protect the man who tried
to kill me?

"It's your Luna instincts," the voice in my head answers.

My Luna instincts? What's that supposed to mean?

"He tried to kill you, yet you have mercy on him?" Rykan
questions.

"I'm still alive and unharmed, so there's no reason to do
this," I say, staring up at him with gentle eyes. He narrows his
eyes at me. He's suspicious of me, but I guess it's understandable.

He then turns back to the man. "You will live. But do this
again, and I'll not hesitate to end you."

He then grabs my hand and leads me back into the house.
He takes me to the couch and sets me down before sitting

down next to me. "Are you okay?"

The underlying concern in his voice surprises me, but I don't voice my surprise because, even though I know nothing about him, his concern for me still causes my heart to flutter.

"I'm all right. Just a little shaken up is all," I admit, looking down.

"I'm sorry," he says, causing my head to snap up to his. "I shouldn't have just let you go like that. I knew that they were doing their morning training, but I just let you walk right into that."

"It's fine," I find myself saying, although I should be angry at him. This stupid bond.

"No, it's not fine, and you know it. You're just saying that because of the bond."

I don't deny it. At least he knows it.

"It's just . . . this is all so new to me. I'm not sure what to do or what to say to you so that you won't get hurt."

"You hurt me earlier," I find myself admitting.

"I know I did, and that's why I'm apologising. I should be more considerate towards you because of the bond. None of this is your fault," he says, sighing deeply.

He looks so truly apologetic that my own heart clenches in my chest. I want to stop this. I want to make him feel better. What can I do? Is there nothing I can give to him?

Then suddenly, the only thing that I can give to him and no one else stares me right in the face. I swallow. Am I really going to do this? Am I ready for this? I barely know him. But as he avoids my eyes, looking regretful, I realise that even if I don't want to, I have to. It's the bond, I know, but still. I can't stop myself.

Without thinking about it twice, I lean forward, pressing my lips against his. This is all I can give him right now.

My first kiss.

CHAPTER EIGHTEEN

Rykan tenses.

His lips are so foreign, yet they feel so soft and so warm. It may just be the bond, but I feel like his lips are meant to touch mine, like we're sealing something together, and I know now. Something has slotted itself in my heart, and I know it's not going anywhere.

Rykan doesn't respond to my kiss, his lips still against mine, and I can't help but bring my hand to his cheek, moving my lips against his. And finally, after a few moments, I pull away.

Rykan looks bewildered, his eyes dazed as he processes what just happened. I touch my fingers to my lips. I can barely believe that just happened myself. What in the world possessed me to kiss him? And first? I must have momentarily lost my mind.

"I'm sorry," I squeak out. "I wasn't thinking."

"Don't ever do that again," he warns, his eyes dark. I nod, swallowing uncomfortably. Then he stands. "Come on. I'll have someone take you home."

I want to ask him why he won't take me home myself, but I control myself. I don't think I should, considering the fact that I just kissed him against his will. Sighing begrudgingly, I stand up.

"Right. Where's my cell phone and my bags?" I ask.

"I'll have them in the car for you," he says, walking out of the house.

I follow him outside, avoiding the stares of the other

werewolves, and within moments, we arrive at a sleek black car parked on a dirt road that I didn't even know the forest had. The driver's seat door opens, and a figure steps out.

"Her bags and everything are in the car," the person says, and I immediately recognise him. Cole.

"Take her home safely," Rykan says, disappearing before I can say a thing.

"Get in," Cole says before getting back into the car. Pursing my lips in frustration, I open the car door and climb into the car, spotting my school bag, duffle bag, and cell phone lying on the backseat. "Where do you live?"

I freeze. I can't go home, no matter what. My father's probably waiting for me there. I can't.

Without another thought, I tell him Lia's address, and he nods, starting the engine and driving.

The drive to Lia's is silent, and we stop in front of her house. I grab my things and get out of the car without a word, slamming the door closed behind me.

"Where the hell have you been?" is the first thing to leave Lia's mouth when I walk through the door.

Not answering her, I drop my bags to the floor and walk into her arms, snuggling my face into her neck.

"What's wrong? Are you okay?"

I sigh. Is it really a good idea to tell Lia everything? Probably not, but I need to talk to someone about it. It's too much to just deal with myself. I need advice, support, and most importantly, I need someone to tell me that everything is going to be okay. Because telling myself that isn't working.

Pulling away from Lia, I lead her to the couch, where we sit down next to each other, and after making sure that her mom isn't anywhere in the vicinity, I tell her *everything*. From Jackson, to passing out, and Rykan. By the time I'm done speaking, Lia's staring at me with wide eyes and a slack jaw. She opens and closes her mouth a few times, but she looks completely speechless. I would be, too, if it hadn't happened to me.

"Are you okay?" she asks, her voice soft.

I hesitate for a moment before I shake my head. I'm not. I'm far from okay.

She immediately pulls me into her arms. "I'm so sorry you had to go through that, Lexi. You really don't deserve it."

Then there's something else I also need to come clean about. My father. "Lia, there's something else I need to tell you, too." I start, pulling away from her. Her eyebrows furrow, but she stays silent, letting me speak finish first. "My father . . . he . . . he abuses me."

There it is. I've said it. I can't take it back now.

"What?" Her eyes are wide. "He . . . what?"

"He abuses me," I say, staring down at my hands.

"Why didn't you say anything?" she asks, sounding small.

"Because I didn't want to burden you with my problems," I admit. "I just felt like it was something I had to deal with alone."

"No," Lia scolds. "How could you ever think that? I'm your best friend, and I want to be here for you no matter what. If you had told me sooner, I never would have let you go to your house every day."

"I'm sorry."

"That's it," she says, sudden determination filling her voice. "You're staying here from now on. I'll talk to my mom, and I'm sure she'll say yes. You're not going back to that house, Lexi."

Relief floods my body. I pull her into another hug, sniffling as tears fill my eyes. "Thank you, Lia."

"But, Lexi," she suddenly says. "What are you going to do about this thing with Rykan? It kind of seems like it's not something you can easily escape."

I don't answer. She's right. In fact, I don't think that there's any way to escape this situation I'm in. And what am I going to do about it?

I have no idea.

CHAPTER NINETEEN

I'm returning to school today, and I'm not looking forward to it.

There are several reasons why I don't want to go to school, the common reasons being the fact that I hate school and studying, but the more unusual reasons being Jackson and Rykan. I'm not sure what Jackson is going to do when I show up today, especially since the mark on my neck no longer belongs to him. Rykan, I don't know. He probably won't even pay a sliver of attention to me.

With a deep breath, I walk through the school doors. I keep my hands wrapped around my schoolbag straps as I walk. This morning, I made sure to splay my hair across my shoulder and neck to cover the bite mark. The last thing I need right now is for someone to see it and get suspicious.

When I walk into the classroom, Lia waves at me, gesturing me to sit down next to her, and I do, forcing a tight-lipped smile onto my face. "How are you feeling so far?"

"Nervous," I admit.

"Well, don't worry. I haven't seen Jackson or Rykan yet. Maybe we'll get lucky and they both just won't show up today," she says. Like that will ever happen.

Luckily, for the rest of the period, Rykan doesn't show up for class. Maybe he'll stay away after all. But as I walk out of my third class of the day, I'm pulled into the janitor's closet. I gasp in surprise, my eyes widening with horror when I see who's pulled me in here.

Jackson.

I open my mouth to scream, but he's quick to cover my mouth with his hand, muffling any sound that escapes my lips.

"Looks like you survived," he says, a wicked smile appearing on his face. "I'm pleased."

He uses his free hand to move my hair out of the way, but the moment his eyes land on my neck, the smile he has on his face disappears.

"What the hell is this?" he roars, making me flinch. His hand slips from my face in his rage. "That's not my mark!"

"You're right," I say, presenting faux confidence. "It's another werewolf's mark. So what? What are you going to do about it?"

He punches his fist into the wall right next to my head. "How dare you challenge me?"

I gulp.

"I'll ask once, and I'll ask nicely, whose mark is this?" he calmly asks, but I purse my lips closed. There's no way I'm telling him. "Tell me!"

"No," I refuse. "I won't tell you a thing."

Then he smirks. "Well then. I guess I just have to force it out of you then."

I'm not sure what he means by that, but I quickly realise when his hand wraps around my throat. Suddenly, images of my father repeatedly choking me flash before my eyes, and I wrap my hands around his wrist, trying to pry him off me, but it doesn't work. As a werewolf, he's far too strong. Then I remember. Rykan said that his bite will make me have special abilities like heightened strength.

With that in mind, I squeeze his wrist as harshly as I can, putting all my strength into it, but I fail. He barely moves an inch. Oh God, what do I do now? How do I activate these special abilities?

Jackson squeezes, slowly choking me until I cough. "If I

were you, I'd start talking."

"You won't hurt me," I choke out. "You told me you have feelings for me. Surely, you won't hurt someone you have feelings for?"

He laughs. "What makes you think that?"

I freeze.

"You must really be confident in my feelings for you," he says, a yellow glow appearing in his eyes. "It's too bad, though, because if it's not my mark on you, I see no point in letting you live just to be someone else's."

My heart drops to my stomach as I realise he's going to kill me.

"You're really going to do that here?" I choke out. "You won't be able to get away with it."

He smiles. "We'll see about that."

Then his grip on my throat tightens, and he's choking me now with the intent of killing me. I cough, oxygen leaving my lungs, and I struggle against him, my knees giving in.

"Please," I choke out. "Please spare me."

He merely smiles, appearing to find pleasure in my pain, his grip tightening even more than I thought possible. I grip his shirt in my hand, my fingers shaky, and within moments, all my will to fight leaves my body, and my hand slips from his shirt, falling to my side.

"Help," I weakly call out. "Rykan."

He's the only one I can think of right now. But chances are he won't help me even if he can hear me. In fact, he'll be happy to be rid of me and our bond.

"Rykan?" Jackson growls. "Is he the werewolf who marked you?"

I've made him even angrier. Great.

"Rykan, help me," I whisper. He's my last hope, even if he doesn't give a damn about me.

My eyelids become weak, and I quickly feel all life being

drained from my body. Suddenly, the door bursts open, and a large figure tackles Jackson to the ground. The moment I'm free from his grip, I gasp for air, sliding down the wall. I can't make out anything clearly in here. Why is the light off during the day?

But luckily I can make out two figures, one lying on the ground with another on top of him, gripping his collar and punching him repeatedly. It feels like such a relief to be able to breathe again, but I can't help but want to stop the fight. Whoever has come here to save me can't kill Jackson. That will only cause trouble for them.

"Hey," I weakly call out. "Stop. You're going to kill him."

But he doesn't stop, repeatedly punching Jackson with the same murderous intent Jackson had merely moments ago.

"You . . . you have to stop." I breathe out. But he still doesn't. Forcing myself to my feet, I rush over to them as fast as I can after what just happened to me, barely thinking before leaning down and wrapping my arms around the person from behind. He freezes, his fist mid-air.

"Stop," I breathlessly say, hugging him. Then a familiar scent enters my nostrils, and I realise who it is. "It's okay, Rykan."

His body eventually relaxes against mine, and he slowly stands up, my arms remaining firmly wrapped around him. Jackson remains on the ground, passed out, I'm assuming. Rykan turns around in my arms, and the movement causes my arms to slip off him. His hand reaches up to cup my cheeks, his body warmth enveloping me.

Then when I look up at him, I notice his molten gold glowing eyes. "You."

His voice, there's something different about it. His voice sounds deeper, raspier.

"Rykan." I breathe out.

"I'm not Rykan," he says.

"Then who are you?" I ask, breathless.

His golden eyes search mine, as if he's looking for something. Then he answers. "I'm Axel."

CHAPTER TWENTY

A *xel.*

Who's Axel? Well, obviously, he's Axel, but how can that be?

As if he can sense my confusion, he says, "I'm Rykan's wolf."

"You're . . . Rykan's wolf?" I slowly ask, and he nods. I read about this somewhere. That a werewolf has another personality of sorts and that it's their wolf, their werewolf side. However, I've never encountered this in real life. I've read stories, but this is a first for me.

"Thank you," I breathe out. "For saving me."

His golden eyes flash. "I heard you. You called for me."

My eyes widen. He heard me? I was sure that he couldn't, but he did.

"You heard me?" I ask, my voice soft. He nods. Tears fill my eyes, and I purse my lips, staring up at him. Then his eyes move down to my neck.

"Did he do that to you?" he says, growling, and I take a step back in caution. His eyes widen at my movement, and he quickly places his hands on my hips and gently tugs me forward into his chest. "Don't be scared of me. I'd never hurt you."

Axel . . . the way he's speaking to me . . . he's so different from Rykan. Rykan is mean and cold, but Axel's caring and gentle towards me. He even saved me from Jackson, something that I feel like Rykan wouldn't have done.

"Do you hate me?" I can't help but ask.

His eyebrows furrow. "Why would you think that?" he questions, his grip on my hips tightening slightly.

"Well . . . Rykan hates me," I mumble, avoiding his eyes. "Especially after I kissed him."

I'm embarrassed to say this, but I feel like it has to be said.

"He doesn't hate you," Axel says. "Trust me."

"He doesn't?" I softly ask, and he nods.

"It must have bothered you, huh?" he says, and I nod, looking down. He immediately grabs my chin, tilting my head upwards. "Look at me."

"But aren't you both angry at me because of the fake mate bond?" I ask, my lips trembling.

"It's not fake," he says, then lightly growls, pulling me closer by my hips. "You saying that it's fake makes me angry."

My eyebrows furrow in confusion. Why would he say that? Isn't our bond just a faux-mate bond? However, I don't argue with him, staying silent.

Then the closet light flickers on, and I turn around slightly. Cole and Gage come rushing in, breathless as though they've been running all over. Their eyes widen at Axel and me.

"Axel, we looked everywhere for you," Gage rushes out, placing his hands on his hips. "You just suddenly stormed out of the cafeteria without saying anything to us."

"We were worried about you," Cole softly says, and the gentleness in his voice surprises me. He always came off as an unaffectionate and cold person, but I guess he's different when it comes to the people he cares about.

"Sorry," I hear Axel say from behind me. Then their eyes flutter to Jackson's unconscious form lying on the ground.

"What happened here?" Gage asks.

"Jackson attacked me," I answer, staring up at them with hesitant eyes. I'm heavily aware that Axel's hands are still on me and that the two of them can see it.

"The bastard tried to kill her." Axel growls.

"And . . . you're angry?" Cole questions, narrowing his eyes at Axel.

"He tried to kill my mate. Why would I not be angry?" Axel says.

My eyes widen, and my head snaps up to his. Did he just call me his . . . mate?

Cole and Gage look just as surprised as I am. Cole clears his throat uncomfortably. "Axel, she's not your real mate."

I look down, my mood deflating. Right, I'm not his real mate. Axel quickly notices how I feel, and he pulls me closer until my face is pressed against his chest, and his arms wrap around my body, as if he's protecting me.

"Shut your mouth, Cole." Axel growls, his voice sounding a lot more dominant than ever before, and Cole immediately cowers, taking a step back and bowing his head slightly.

"Axel," Gage calls out. "You should give Rykan his control back. It's dangerous for you to be in control at school for any-one to see."

Axel sighs, his eyes meeting mine. His hand touches my cheek, cupping as his molten gaze softens. "My mate, we will meet again."

He called me his mate again. What does this mean?

Suddenly, he's leaning down. His lips soon meet mine, and my eyes widen. It's soft and quick. And when his eyes open, they've returned to their usual chocolate-brown colour. He immediately pulls away from me, taking a few steps away from me.

I realise Rykan has returned.

"Rykan," Gage calls out. Rykan's eyes are wide as he shakes out of his trance.

"Huh?" he distractedly mutters.

"Are you okay?" Gage asks, staring at Rykan in concern. Rykan's eyes flutter to mine.

"No," he answers. "I'm not okay."

Then he's out the door. Gage and Cole spare me one last glance before rushing out after Rykan.

With a sigh, I turn back to Jackson's unconscious body.

What do I do now?

CHAPTER TWENTY-ONE

Rykan

I'm not okay.

I'm far from okay. I can't believe what just happened. After everything I did to push Lexia away and keep a distance between us, Axel ruined it within one moment. What was he even thinking? She's not our mate, so why did he treat her like she is? Why did he hold her like that? Why did he get so angry at the thought of another man touching her? Why did he kiss her?

"Rykan!" I hear a voice call out from behind me, and I come to a stop. "Rykan, what the hell just happened?"

I turn to Cole and Gage with a frustrated groan, dragging my fingers through my hair.

"Rykan . . ." Gage trails off, concern swirling in his eyes. He's worried for me.

"Guys . . . I don't know," I say with a light sigh.

"Why did Axel behave in that way? And why did he call her your mate?" Cole persists, and even though Gage gives him a look to stop, he doesn't. "Tell us the truth, Rykan."

"I don't know, Cole!" I exclaim, ruffling my hair atop my head. "I don't know why Axel did what he did. But just know, it wasn't me. I would never do that."

"He seems to care for her," Gage softly notes.

"I know, and I don't understand why. It's not like she's our real mate. This fake mate bond wasn't supposed to affect us," I say.

"Don't you dare call it a fake bond!"

I sigh as Axel's angered voice resonates through my head. *"She's our mate."*

"She's not our mate." I can't help but growl, startling my two friends. Axel is really starting to make me angry. First, he touches her, and then he kisses her. There's a line, and he crossed it.

"Stop trying to deny it. You feel it, don't you?"

"I don't feel anything."

"Liar. I'm a part of you. You can't lie to me."

"Stop this. Stop trying to convince me that there's something between Lexia and I when there isn't."

"Rykan, I know that we've been hurt by humans before, but this is different. I know you can feel it."

"Just stop."

"But I'm not wrong."

"Just shut up and go away."

"Rykan, just listen to me — "

"Go away!"

I close off my mind, shutting him out. He's wrong. Lexia isn't our mate, and she isn't different. She's just like every other evil human being who preys on werewolves. I'll never accept her. I'll never let her in. It's in this moment that I wish I just let her die. No, I should've walked away from her when she was in trouble in the first place. Then she would've died, and I wouldn't have known about it.

Why did I hesitate, though? Why did seeing her so afraid make my heart ache? No, I need to stop thinking about this. I have to stop before I start thinking like Axel does.

Shaking off my thoughts, I bring my attention back to Cole and Gage.

"What does Axel say?" Cole asks, already knowing that I zoned out because I was having a conversation with my wolf.

"He's convinced Lexia is our mate," I say with hesitation, unsure of how the two of them will react.

"Don't you think there's a reason for that?" Gage softly asks, as if he's afraid his words will tick me off.

"What possible reason could there be for this?" Cole says, glaring at Gage for merely uttering those words. "Axel is just going through a phase because he's frustrated that after eighteen years of existing, he still hasn't found his mate. This girl is merely a substitute to make himself feel better."

"He's wrong. Lexia's no substitute!"

"Go away, Axel!"

I'm not sure how he did it, but he managed to break through the walls around my mind, and he sounds even angrier than earlier.

"That's how strong my feelings are for her. Not even you can keep me out."

"What is he saying now?" Cole grumbles, unimpressed.

"The same," I defeatedly say. "He's angry at you now."

"What the hell is wrong with him?" Cole says. "Of all people, he should be the one encouraging you not to fall for a human, not the other way around."

"Cole, calm down," Gage softly says. "Getting angry is not the solution."

"Well then, what do you suggest?" Cole questions, folding his arms across his chest.

"Let's just stay calm and just ignore Lexia if we do come across her, okay," Gage says, and I nod, already done with this conversation. Gage is right. Getting angry won't solve anything. If anything, it'll make things worse. We all just need to calm down.

"You, too, Axel."

I hear Axel grumble in my mind, and I smile, knowing that I've won this argument.

"It's time for PE. Let's go and blow off some steam," Cole says, stretching out his arms behind him as he starts walking in the direction of the field. Gage and I follow behind him to the field. The rest of our class is already there when we arrive.

I ignore their stares, and I'm not in the mood to deal with them right now.

"All right, is everyone here?" Coach Davis yells out, and in that exact moment, Lexia comes running onto the field, muttering a soft apology when coach glares at her. Why is she here? She was just attacked. Shouldn't she be resting or something?

I don't fail to notice the lack of a bruise around her throat. Thanks to my bite, she's already healed. I watch her as she walks over to her friend, Lia, I think. I remember her. She was the girl who dared to speak against me on the first day, and she was the one with Lexia in the forest that night. I'm guessing she was the one who convinced Lexia to go into the forest in the first place. She looks like that type who forces their soft-spoken friends to do something they don't want to.

Not that I care. If Lexia wants to associate with someone like that, that's her problem.

"All right, we're going to start with three laps around the field. Let's go!" Coach Davis yells out, blowing his whistle. We all start running, the heat barely bothering me as I run across the field with ease. However, I quickly catch sight of a frantic body running across the field without control. Lexia.

Her new abilities have been activated with our kiss from earlier, and now she's struggling to control it. She may even hurt herself at the rate that she's going. Three laps end quickly, but by the time everyone's stopped, she's still running, her face panic-stricken as she appears to be internally praying for help.

"Help her."

I roll my eyes at Axel's words. *"Why should I help her?"*

"Because you're the only one who can."

I ignore him.

"Please, Rykan."

The pleading in Axel's voice startles me. He never begs for anything, not even for control.

"She's going to hurt herself."

"And why should I care?"

"Because she's our mate. I don't care about what you think any-more. Whether it be a real mate bond or a fake one, she remains our mate, so help her."

My fingers twitch at my sides.

"I know you want to."

He's right, but why? *"Why do I want to help her?"*

"Because you feel what I feel, too."

"Please. Someone help me," I hear Lexia faintly whisper under her breath. That's the last thing it takes for me to go running after her, ignoring Cole and Gage's yells behind me. I stop a few metres in front of her, holding my arms out to her. Her eyes widen when she sees me, and she quickly gestures for me to get out of the way, but I don't. And soon, she comes crashing into me.

I catch her in my arms, using my strength to stop myself from falling backwards and balancing the two of us. Then our eyes meet. There it is again. That innocent and hesitant gaze that she always looks at me with. Her eyes — they're brown, yet they're so green, so beautiful, and finally, I allow myself to think about her in the way that I've been forcing myself not to since I first met her.

She's beautiful, so beautiful that it hurts.

CHAPTER TWENTY-TWO

He's beautiful, so beautiful that it hurts.
Now that I'm so close to him and I can finally see everything up close, I realise how truly ethereal he is. It's almost as
if he's not even supposed to exist.

And he's staring down at me. However, the look in his eyes
is different. He's looking at me differently. For the first time
ever, he's not glaring at me or holding a coldness in his eyes,
but there's something else. Something warmer, almost.

"Are you okay?" he asks, pulling me out of my thoughts. I
nod, staring up at him with big eyes.

"What . . . what just happened to me?" I softly mutter, confused as to what just happened. I was running faster than I've
ever run before, but then I couldn't stop. I tried, but my body
just kept on going without control. Who knows what might
have happened if Rykan hadn't stepped in and helped me?

"It's because of your new abilities the bond gave you.
You're faster now, much faster," he says.

Is that what it was?

"How . . . how do I control it?" I can't help but ask.

"With training, it should get easier," he says, although his
words do nothing to calm my nerves.

Training. Where in the world am I supposed to get training? And somehow, I doubt that it's training I can get at the
gym. My mood deflates, my lips forming a little pout which
Rykan quickly notices.

"What's wrong?"

"Where am I supposed to get training for these new

abilities?" I mumble, looking down.

Rykan doesn't respond. However, his body tenses against mine. Sighing, I look down, and then I notice something. Why does my chest look like that?

My hand flies to my upper back, and my eyes widen in realisation. My bra shot loose.

Oh no. My eyes move up to Rykan's, and I immediately push him away, taking a few steps away from him. He looks startled by my sudden action, but I can hardly care, wrapping my arms around my chest.

"Look away," I say.

"What—"

"I said look away!" I say, and he quickly turns around in his spot.

"What's . . . what's the matter?" he hesitantly asks, but I ignore him, turning around and rushing away from him. I can only hope he didn't feel anything when I was pressed up against him.

"What's wrong?" Lia asks when I rush up to her, my face panicky.

"My bra shot loose," I quietly say so that no one but her can hear me.

"Well, I'm not surprised," she says, although this confuses me. "With all the running you were doing earlier, I'd be surprised if it stayed intact."

"Just help me," I say, pulling her to the side, away from everyone else. I then turn my back to her. However, when her fingers fiddle with the strap for a few moments and it doesn't get tied, I turn around. "What are you doing?"

"You know I don't wear bras, so I've never done this before," she says, and I sigh. "I mean, how tight is tight enough so that I don't end up killing you?"

"The second hoop," I say, turning around again. Lia sighs, but just as her fingers touch the hem of my sweater, three figures come up to us. My eyes widen, and I'm quickly to shove her hands away.

"Hi, Lia," Gage greets, flashing her a smile. Her eyes light up.

"Oh, hi, Gage. Long time no chat," she says, her voice sweet.

"Hi . . . Lexia, right?" Gage greets, his eyes fluttering to mine.

"That's me," I say, awkwardly pointing at myself. I'm pretty sure he knows my name, considering what's happened between Rykan and me, but I don't question him. He may just be doing this to emphasize the fact that I'm no one of importance. That sucks. Then my eyes move to Cole, who just awkwardly stands there, glaring at me. "Hi, Cole."

He just scoffs, turning his face away from me. I purse my lips, ignoring his attitude. I mean, what did I expect?

"All right, everyone," Coach Davis yells out, grabbing our attention. "Grab a partner. We're going to be doing some exercises now."

"Lia?" Gage calls out, holding his hand out to her. She's quick to take his hand and let him lead her away, flashing me a smile as she goes. That just leaves Rykan, Cole, and me, but when I turn to Cole, he merely sends me one last glare before walking away. Now it's just Rykan and me.

Should I ask him to be my partner? That's probably not a good idea since I'm almost a hundred per cent certain he hates me. However, just as I'm about to walk away from him, his hand wraps around my wrist, and he pulls me back.

"Let's be partners."

I blink in surprise, once, twice. Did he just . . .

"Why?" I blurt out, my eyes widening once I realise I just made it sound like I have a problem with being partners with him when I don't. Ever since the beginning of our bond, I've wanted nothing more than to be close to him.

"Why?" he repeats. "Well . . . why not?"

Yeah, why not?

Smiling up at him, I nod. He then slides his hand down my wrist to my hand and wraps it around my fingers. My heart stutters at the feeling of him holding my hand, and I smile stupidly up at him as he pulls me onto the field. We stop at an open spot. However, I don't fail to notice that he's led me to a spot away from everyone else. I don't question why, though. It might just be because he wants to avoid having to listen to our classmates gossip about him.

He sits down on the grass, pulling me down to sit opposite him. He doesn't let go of my hand, though, rubbing his thumb across my palm. He's being oddly affectionate, and even though I like this side of him, it's strange. I can't help but think what if he's being this way on purpose because he's about to drop yet another bomb on me that will potentially break my heart.

"All right, so we'll start with some stretches. Do any stretches you wish to do. You have five minutes," Coach Davis says, blowing his whistle. I think he likes blowing that whistle a little too much. I remember once I was standing right next to him when he blew the whistle, and I'm pretty sure I went temporarily deaf.

"So," Rykan starts, letting go of my hand. "What exercises do you want to do?"

I hum. "I don't really exercise besides when it's PE, so I don't really know any stretches. What do you suggest?"

He smirks, a mischievous glint appearing in his eyes. It surprises me because, for the first time, his face is not stone-cold and emotionless. What's happened to change him so drastically?

"Well, I have a couple of stretches in mind," he murmurs, and I narrow my eyes at him in suspicion. Then suddenly, he falls back onto the grass, and he pulls me forward by my hands, causing me to fall on top of him, our faces merely inches apart.

My eyes widen at our close proximity, my heart beating wildly against my ribs. Rykan places his hands on my hips, gripping the material of my shorts tightly. I suck in a breath, focusing on the golden specks in his eyes. Is it just me or have they become more apparent?

"Amaris," he whispers, brushing his lips against mine.

That name . . . it feels like mine. No, it *is* mine.

"Kiss me, Rykan," I murmur against his lips, and that's all it takes for him to delve his hand into my hair, pressing his lips against to mine, finally. I kiss him harder, his name leaving my lips in a breathless moan.

I don't care if anyone can see the two of us right now. All I care about is him and savouring this moment. I never want this to end.

"Lexia," he breathes.

Lexia?

My eyes snap open, only to find Rykan staring down at me with furrowed eyebrows. I look around. The two of us are alone, but we're still standing at our previous spot. Oh no, did I imagine us being partners and us . . . kissing?

Dread fills me.

"What's wrong?" he asks, reaching out to me, but I pull away, taking a few steps back before I run away.

What's wrong with me?

CHAPTER TWENTY-THREE

"I love you, Amaris."

The way he whispers my name, it's filled with desire. His hand gently brushes my cheek, across my cheekbone. He's so close to me. I can feel him and his desire. I wish I could see him, but everything is dark. All I can focus on is his presence, his touch, and his smell.

His scent . . . it's familiar, yet so foreign. It feels as though I've smelled it before, yet it also feels like the first time. Who is this man?

"I love you, too," I barely whisper. I can feel it in my heart, in my entire being. I love this man with everything in me, but I want to see him. I want to see his face. I want to stroke his skin. I want to kiss him.

"Lexia, wake up," I hear a voice yell out. Lexia, who's that? "Lexia!"

My eyes snap open. They immediately focus on my surroundings, and I quickly realise that I'm in Lia's bedroom. Lia sighs. "Finally. I've been trying to wake you for so long now."

What's going on? Why am I here? What just happened . . . was it all a dream? Who was that man, and why did he call me Amaris? The only person who calls me Amaris is the voice in my head, so what was that?

"Come on. You have ten minutes to get ready, and if you're not done in time, I'm leaving you here," Lia says before leaving the room.

I'm so confused, but I shake off all my thoughts and get up from the bed. I can think about that later. For now, in the present, I need to get ready for school.

114

I take a quick shower before slipping into my school uniform and sneakers and meeting Lia downstairs. She smiles at me when I reach her, and then we leave her house and start our walk to school. It's been a week since I've officially started living with Lia and her mom, and so far, it's been great. I don't have to dread going home after school anymore. I always have a hot plate of food at night, and best of all, Vanessa doesn't hit me. To me, this is bliss.

Also, ever since the incident on the field, I've been actively avoiding Rykan and his werewolf friends. Well, at least besides when we have the same classes, which, to my dismay, is more than I initially thought. Usually, when the bell rings, I'm the first one out, and that's saying something. Whether or not Rykan has tried to approach me during this time, I have no idea, although I doubt it. He has no reason to approach me. If anything, he should be glad that I'm no longer around and annoying him.

The thought that he may be relieved to have me out of his life hurts, but I try not to let myself get distracted by it. After all, it's all just because of the bond.

When we arrive at school, Lia and I walk straight to homeroom for our first class. We're first to arrive, and we take our seats and chat about meaningless things while we wait for Ms Blake to arrive.

"So," Lia says, holding up two lipsticks. "Which one do you think matches my skin tone the best?"

I hum in thought. "I think they both go really well with your skin tone."

"But if you had to choose one . . ." she says, insisting.

"Well . . . I guess the deep pink one. The nude one blends in too well with your tanned skin," I say, and she nods, tossing the nude-coloured lipstick into her make-up bag and opening the other one before applying it to her lips.

When she's done, she clips it closed and is about to place it

115

into her make-up bag, but then she turns to me and holds it out to me. "Why don't you try it?"

I shake my head. "No. Make-up's not for me."

"Oh, come on," she whines. "It's just lipstick. It's not like I'm asking you to put on a full face of foundation, concealer, and highlighter."

Pursing my lips, I nod, taking the lipstick from her. I take her small mirror and open the lipstick. I then drag the lipstick across my lips. However, a body bumps into mine from behind, causing me to drag the lipstick across my cheek. I cringe when I see how I look in the mirror.

"Oh, Lexi," Lia says, although I can see the amusement in her eyes. She then takes out a tissue and hands it to me. Grumbling, I bring the tissue to my face, but just as I'm about to wipe the lipstick off my face, I hear a laugh.

I turn my head, and my eyes widen when I see Rykan, Cole, and Gage standing about a metre away from us. Gage is covering his mouth with his hand as he laughs. "You're not very good with make-up, are you?"

"Someone bumped into me!" I pout instinctively.

He holds his hands up in defence. "If you say so, Lexia."

I lean back in my seat, and that's when I notice Rykan staring down at me, a slight quirk to his lips. I'm surprised at the gentleness in his eyes. It's the first time he's stared at me like this, well, when it's not out in a dream.

I'm not sure how long we just stay in our spots, staring at one another like no one else exists, and in this moment, my heart swells in my chest, a certain warmth that I've never felt before enveloping me. I feel . . . different. I know that it's the bond, but still. How can it merely be a by-product of the bond when it feels this real?

Does he feel it, too? That's such a stupid thought. Of course he doesn't. From the beginning, he made it very clear that the bond won't affect him. However, at times—at most times—I find myself hoping, wishing that maybe, just maybe, he can feel a little something for me, too.

"Rykan," Cole says, breaking through our moment. Rykan's eyes leave mine, snapping to Cole. "Let's go."

He then grabs onto Rykan's arm and pulls him to their seats.

Sighing sadly, I look down, but Lia quickly nudges me, her eyes lit up in curiosity. "What just happened? Did you two just have a . . . moment?"

"It wasn't like that." I say defensively. The only reason why did is because I'm trying to convince myself that it was indeed not like I'm hoping.

"I don't believe you," she says, leaning back while narrowing her eyes at me. "Something changed between the two of you."

"Changed? What could have changed?" I scoff, avoiding her eyes.

"Lexi," she whispers, leaning in closer to me. "I thought you said he wouldn't get affected by the bond."

I nod, and she bites her lower lip as she tilts her head to the side. "I don't think so."

"What do you mean?" I can't help but ask.

"I think that he's starting to feel something for you," she secretly whispers, and I burst out laughing. She glares at me, gesturing for me to quiet down. "I'm not joking. I genuinely think he's starting to like you."

I stop laughing, becoming serious. "You really think so?"

She nods, an excited smile appearing on her face. Excitement creeps in, and I can't help but squeal, interlocking our fingers together. We both squeal, not caring about how loud we are being, and Lia then pulls me into her arms, stroking my back. "You see, I don't think the universe hates you after all."

Then I become acutely aware of the fact that the person

we've been talking about this entire time is in the room with us and is a werewolf with sharpened senses. He probably heard everything we've just said.

I slump against Lia, my mood deflating. Lia quickly notices the change in me, and she grips my arms. "Lexi. Lexi, what's wrong?"

"We suck," I mutter, resting my chin on her shoulder.

"What?" Lia asks, confusion lacing her voice.

"Stupid," I said, hitting my forehead on her shoulder. "So stupid."

"You're not stupid," the voice in my head says.

"How do you know that?" I ask.

"You're just lovesick. It's an illness, not stupidity," the voice says, and I can't help but laugh, whining through my laugh.

"Will he ever like me back?" I ask, my voice soft.

There's silence. I sigh. Of course the voice doesn't speak to me when I really want, no, need it to. Then, as if feeling my distress, the voice speaks again.

"He already does."

CHAPTER TWENTY-FOUR

I don't have to do this.

No, I do. Actually, I don't. Why did I even think this was a good idea in the first place? I must've temporarily lost my mind after what the voice in my head said to me. I mean, why did I even believe what the voice said for a second? It's literally just a voice in my own head.

I'm so dumb.

An arm slings across my shoulder. "You can do this, Lexi."

"No, I can't," I whine, turning to Lia. "I really can't."

"Lexi, I told you," she says, lightly scolding. "He likes you, or he's at least starting to like you. It's time for you to make your move."

Taking a deep breath, I nod. I can do this. Hopefully, he does feel something for me, and I don't end up embarrassing myself. Although there's a bigger chance that I'm wrong, and he'll hate me even more after this. But Lia's right. I need to take a chance and make my move before I regret not doing anything when I have the chance.

"You can do it," Lia encourages. "Good luck."

"Wait," I blurt out, my eyes wide. "Are you not coming with me?"

"Why should I? I'm not the one trying to catch a guy," she says.

"But still," I whine, pouting. "You can't just send me there alone."

Lia sighs, but luckily, she nods, taking my arm in her hand. "I'll support you. Let's go."

119

She then leads me to the table where Rykan, Cole, and Gage are sitting, eating their lunch. When we reach their table, Lia purposefully clears her throat, grabbing their attention. They all look up, surprise flashing in their eyes upon seeing us. Lia smiles, pinching my arm, wanting me to open my mouth, but as I stare at the three of them, anxiousness fills me, and I can't seem to move my lips, nor my limbs.

"Lexi," Lia whispers, nudging me. "Say something."

I purse my lips, frozen in my spot. Luckily, noticing my struggle, Lia comes to my rescue.

"Gage, we haven't spoken since that PE class last week, and I was hoping we could catch up," she smoothly lies. Suspicion flashes in his eyes, but he nods nonetheless, and she takes a seat next to him. I, however, remain rooted in my spot. "Oh, you don't mind my bestie sitting with us, too, right?"

Gage hesitantly nods while Cole looks like he wants to throw a tantrum. I'm quick to take a seat next to Lia, and luckily being the furthest seat from Cole. I avoid his glaring eyes, already knowing how angry he must be because if there is one person who hates me more than Rykan, it's Cole.

"So, how have you guys been?" Lia asks, an air of confidence in her voice. She makes up for the confidence that I lack and then some.

"Good," Gage answers. "How about you two?"

"Well, we have both been great," Lia answers with a smile, and then her eyes light up, as if she has just thought of something brilliant. "Oh! But things have been even better for Lexi. She's got a date tonight."

My eyes widen, and my head snaps to hers. What's she doing?

"A date?" Rykan slowly asks, speaking for the first time. I can't help but eye his reaction. How he reacts will tell me how he truly feels about me.

Lia nods. "Yep. He's quite the cutie."

"And why are you telling us this?" Rykan questions through his gritting teeth. Oh my, does this mean . . .

"No reason. I just thought you'd be interested," she nonchalantly says. "I mean, I can imagine you, of all people, want Lexi to find someone and fall in love."

My eyes widen at her words. No, she's going too far. They don't know that she knows what they are.

He narrows his eyes at her. "And why would you think that?"

Lia smirks, leaning her chin on her hand as she stares at Rykan. "Don't you want her not to fall in love with you?"

"And why would she fall in love with me in the first place?" he asks.

He's challenging her, I can tell. *Lia, please don't give me away. I'm trying to get him to fall for me, not hate me even more.*

Lia leans back in her seat. "Well, because you're so handsome, of course."

I release a breath of relief. I knew she wouldn't be as stupid as to blurt out everything that could possibly get me killed.

Rykan leans back in his chair, folding his arms across his chest. His face is stoic as he stares at her. "I don't believe you."

"Believe what you want. Although, I'm not lying. I was attracted to you, too, and wanted to sleep with you once upon a time until you revealed the fact that I'm not a virgin to everyone in our class," she says.

I choke at her words, my eyes widening. Oh no, Lia's getting angry.

"Lia . . ." I trail off, touching my hand to her arm, but she shrugs me off.

"In fact, there's something I'd like to know about you, too," she says, leaning forward.

"And what may that be?" he asks, his voice alarmingly calm.

"Are you even a virgin yourself?" she asks, and my heart

stops, my eyes instinctively moving to Rykan, awaiting his answer. Please. Please let him be —

"No."

His answer has my heart dropping to my stomach. He's not a virgin. Why does that hurt so much?

Lia's eyes widen as she realises what she's just done. Her head snaps to mine, but I look down, avoiding her eyes. My eyes water, and I have to bite my lower lip to stop the tears from rolling down my cheeks.

Standing up abruptly, I say, "I have to go."

I move to rush away, but just as I want to, a large figure appears in front of me, the scent telling me that it's Rykan. I don't dare look up at him, saying, "Get out of the way."

"No," he says defiantly.

Releasing a breath in frustration, I say, "Get out of my way, Rykan."

"No," he repeats. "Not until you look at me."

I force my gaze up to meet his, glaring at him with tear-filled eyes. His eyes widen at my now visible emotions. I force the following words out of my mouth, even though I want nothing more than for him to hold me and comfort me. "Now get lost."

I move to walk around him, but he's quicker than me, his arms wrapping around me and pulling me into his hard chest. I freeze, my eyes widening in shock. "What . . . what are you doing?"

"I'm sorry," he says, his arms around me tightening. "I knew that because of the bond anything like that would hurt you, but I didn't think. I'm really sorry. I didn't mean to hurt you, Lexia."

And that's all it takes for tears to escape my eyes and stream down my face. I don't hug him back, just lean my head against his chest, allowing him to hold me. I don't know what's wrong with me. Why does the mere fact that he's not a virgin cause me to burst into tears? Stupid bond. Stupid Rykan. Stupid everything.

"You don't like me, do you?" I mumble into his chest. He tenses up, and his lack of a response gives me an answer. He really doesn't like me. Why did I ever think that he did?

However, just as I want to pull away from him, his grip on me tightens, and he pulls me even closer. "Honestly, I don't know, Lexia."

What's that supposed to mean? Does it mean that he's not sure whether he likes me or not?

I may be stupid for this, but my heart feels a little lighter in my chest at his words. Maybe, just maybe, there's a chance that he can still start to like me.

"Do you like me?" he asks.

I nod with no hesitation at all. Right now, I don't know if I just like him because of the bond or if my feelings for him run deeper than that, but what I do know is that I like him, a lot more than I initially thought I would.

When I first found out about our bond, I thought that it would merely be a surface-level attraction, but it's so much more than that. I know that this isn't good. I don't know him at all, and he most probably hates me. If it wasn't for the bond, he wouldn't even look twice at me, but for now, that's okay.

In this very moment, I just want to focus on the right now, on the present, and not worry about the future. For once, I just want to get what I want.

"How much do you like me?" Rykan asks.

"A lot," I answer honestly. There's no point in me lying to him because, at this point, he already knows everything. Even if I lie to him, he'll see right through me. That's how much I like him.

"Can't you try to like me?" I mumble, feeling ashamed for asking. *When did I become this pitiful?*

He doesn't answer.

CHAPTER TWENTY-FIVE

I wake up in Rykan's arms.

My eyes tiredly search to my surroundings, and I quickly realise that I'm in the nurse's room. I'm lying on one of the beds with Rykan next to me, his arms wrapped firmly around mine as his chin rests on my head, his eyes closed.

Soft breaths escape his lips as he sleeps, fanning my skin. I subtly shift in his arms, moving so that I can stare at his face. He's really so beautiful, even more so when he doesn't have that permanent scowl on his face. He looks so much better now, so peaceful. I smile, touching his hair with my hand. I softly smooth my hand over his soft hair—his hair that's so much softer than I could have ever imagined.

Now that he's so close, I can finally take a good look at him. His body is so big that it completely engulfs mine, his lips so pink, and his long eyelashes that fan his face. He's so perfect I can hardly believe he's real.

He groans slightly, shifting, his arms around me tightening, and then suddenly, his eyes flutter open, meeting mine. I immediately look away, my cheeks flushing in embarrassment that I got caught staring. I never openly stare at males, yet the one time I do, I get caught.

"Lexia," he calls out, his voice deep and raspy from sleep. The sound has me weak in the knees, and if I wasn't laying down already, I'd be on the floor. He reaches out, his fingers grazing my cheek. "So beautiful."

The heat in my cheeks deepens at his words, and I shyly avoid his eyes. The effect he has on me is too strong for me to handle.

"How are you feeling now?" he asks.

"I feel better, I guess." I shrug. He hums, brushing my hair out of my face. "Rykan, can I ask you something?"

He nods, paying more attention to my hair than my face. I have a feeling I'll regret asking this question, but it's bothering me, and I need to get it out.

"How many women have you been with?" I blurt out, avoiding his eyes when they snap to mine.

"Is that really important?" he asks, his hand stilling. I gulp.

"I guess not," I say with a defeated sigh.

"Not that many," he eventually says. "I mean, I'm only eighteen years old."

I nod, knowing that's the most accurate answer I'm going to get from him.

Not thinking, I snuggle more into him, and he laughs, the sound causing me to freeze.

"Did you just laugh?" I ask, looking up at him.

"Yes," he answers. "Is that so . . . surprising?"

"Yes, of course it is," I exclaim, sitting up. "Usually, you're so stoic and emotionless. You never smile, and you always look so angry at the world."

He leans back into the pillow, his eyes searching my face.

"What?" I question.

"Nothing. It's just . . . this is the first time I've seen you look so happy since I met you," he says, making me realise that he's right.

"Well, I didn't have much to be happy about," I say with a shrug.

"And now?" he asks.

"Now . . . now I have you," I say, smiling shyly at him. He doesn't say anything, just staring blankly at me. I hate that blank stare of his.

Suddenly, he sits up, his hand cupping my cheek and his

lips meeting mine. My eyes widen in surprise. He's . . . he's kissing me voluntarily for the first time. My eyes flutter closed, and I kiss him back, and my word, it's amazing.

Kissing him . . . it's so much better out of my imagination or dream.

He deepens the kiss, his tongue swiping across my lips before delving into my mouth in a way that has my toes curling in my shoes. I wrap my arms around his neck, pulling him closer. His hands move down to my hips where he stops, gripping the material of my school shirt in a way that tells me he wants it off.

I pull away to take a breath, gasping when his lips meet the sensitive skin of my neck, placing wet kisses all over my warm skin. His lips trail down to my collarbone and where my shirt buttons stop before he lifts his head and stares hazily at me, his lips swollen from our kiss. I'm sure I look the same.

"What . . . what was that for?" I mumble, my cheeks flushing as an aftermath of what we just did.

"I just wanted to kiss you so badly in that moment," he admits, his sudden confession causing my eyes to widen in shock. He laughs, reaching out to caress my cheek with his hand. "You're so beautiful. Do you know that?"

"Really?" I hesitantly ask. I've never considered myself to be beautiful, so hearing this from him comes as a first for me. He nods, a certain gentleness overtaking his face as he stares at me.

He then grasps my face in between his hands, leaning in closer, murmuring, "Pretty baby."

Then he kisses me again.

Chapter Twenty-Six

For the first time ever, I'm happy to go to school.

And there's only one reason for that. Rykan. After yesterday, I can't wait to see him again, and that's why I stand at the bottom of the staircase, yelling at Lia every two minutes. Finally, after what feels like forever, she comes running down the stairs, her shoes untied.

"I'm here, geez. So in a hurry to meet lover boy?" she teases, leaning down to tie her shoes. I merely laugh, not disagreeing with her since she's not exactly wrong.

"Come on," I whine, grabbing her arm and pulling her out the door with me. I skip all the way to school, excitement filling my body when we walk through the school gates. However, the excitement quickly dissipates, and dread replaces it when I see a familiar figure leaning against his car in the school parking lot, his eyes set on me.

My smile is instantly replaced with a frown. What's he doing here?

"Lexi, let's go," Lia hurriedly says to me, pulling on my arm, but before I can move a single inch, he calls out my name.

He comes stomping over to us, and fear creeps in, leaving my limbs frozen in place. Lia quickly notices and squeezes my arm before saying, "I'll go get Rykan." Then she rushes into the school.

He stops in front of me. "It's been a while, Lexia."

"What are you doing here, Father?" I question, glaring at him.

"Is that how you greet your father, who you haven't seen

for days?" he asks, and I scoff.

"What do you want?" I say.

"I've gotten permission from your school to take you with me," he says, smiling down at me.

Dread fills me, and my eyes widen. "I'm not going anywhere with you."

"Well, too bad you don't have a choice, girlie," he taunts, grabbing my wrist.

"Let go of me!" I yell out, pulling against his grip on me.

"Enough!" he yells out, pulling me against him so that he can whisper into my ear. "Unless you want me to beat you right here in front of everyone, you'll come with me silently."

I clench my hand into a fist, pursing my lips. I have to go with him now. I have no choice.

Unclenching my fist, I let him pull me to the car. He forces me into the passenger seat, buckling me in before getting into the driver's seat and starting the car. Two familiar figures come rushing out of the school doors.

Lia and Rykan.

I bite my lower lip as tears threaten to escape my eyes. I want to go back to them. I want to rush back into Rykan's safe and warm arms. But I can't.

My father reverses out of the parking bay and drives to the school gates. I know that once we drive through them, it's over for me. I can't help but wish and pray and hope that by some miracle, I'll be saved before then.

Then, as if an angel from above has heard my earnest pleads, suddenly, just as we're about to drive through the school gates, a body appears in front of the car, placing their hands against the car's bonnet and stopping the car. Both my father and I fall forward from the impact, my head hitting the dashboard hard. I wince in pain, my hand moving up to my head. When I lift my eyes, I peer over the smoke that escapes the bonnet from the impact. My eyes widen when the smoke clears, and the figure becomes clear to me.

Rykan.

His eyes are dark as he releases his hands from the bonnet, a frown apparent on his face. Relief floods my body. He came. He came to save me.

"What the hell?" My father grunts from beside me, but my eyes remain on Rykan, who now rounds the car and rips open the passenger side car door. All I can do is watch as he leans down, unbuckling the seatbelt before his arms wrap around my form, and he lifts me up and out of the car.

"Are you okay?" Rykan worriedly questions, his eyes scanning over every inch of my body, but instead of answering him, I just stare up at him, stuck in a daze. His eyes meet mine again, and his eyebrows furrow in concern. "Lexia? Lexia?"

I snap out of my daze, blinking before nodding at his previous question.

He releases a breath of relief, his eyes fluttering closed for a slight moment. Then his eyes move up, and when they land on my forehead, he frowns. "You're bleeding."

I look down at my hand that I previously held on my head and notice the red liquid that's stained the tips of my fingers. Blood.

"Hey!" my father yells out, grabbing both our attention. When we turn to him, he's glaring heavily at Rykan. "What the hell do you think you're doing?"

As if by instinct, Rykan pulls me into him, his arm wrapped firmly around my waist. By now, a crowd has formed around us and the car, having witnessed the entire scene. I press myself even more into Rykan's hold, as if he can protect me from everyone's stares.

"You tried to kidnap her," Rykan says.

"Kidnap her? She's my daughter. How is that kidnapping?" my father asks.

"It's kidnapping when she's not going willingly," Rykan

says back.

My father laughs, although all that underlies in his laugh is bitterness.

"Rykan," I call out softly, and his eyes snap down to mine, the previous harshness in them disappearing. "Can you please not make a scene? Everyone's watching."

His eyes flutter to the crowd before meeting mine again, and he nods, turning back to my father. "Leave, now."

"I'm not leaving without my daughter," my father firmly says.

A frustrated sigh escapes me. He's not backing down. He won't stop. He won't leave until I get into his car. And I can't. No, I won't. Rykan came here to help me, to save me from my abusive father, so I won't just admit defeat like I usually do. I have to fight back.

"Just stop!" I yell out, glaring at my father. "That's enough, Father."

"Keep your mouth shut, Lexia." my father warns.

"No, I won't," I say. "I won't keep quiet any longer. I'm done, okay. I'm sick of this. I'm sick of being treated like your punching bag. What happened to Mom . . . that wasn't my fault, and I shouldn't get punished for it. I took it all, all these years. I took all your beatings and never complained or fought back once. I never told anyone about it. Even when I could've reported you, I didn't because I believed in you. I believed that you would change and that everything would be okay again, but I was wrong. After all these years, you haven't changed, and you never will. You'll always remain the same child abuser who forces their own child to entertain his friends' needs."

Rykan tenses against me after I utter those last words, and I know why. He doesn't know about that. No one does.

By the time I'm done talking my heart out, everyone's eyes are wide, and they look beyond shocked by what I've just revealed. I wasn't planning on revealing this today, or ever, but now that I have, I don't regret it. In fact, I'm glad to let it all out.

"You . . . how dare you?" my father yells out, his eyes wide and his jaw slacked. He can't believe what just happened either.

"I would suggest you leave before someone calls the police to report you for child abuse," Rykan says from behind me. My father looks around at all the students surrounding us, and when he sees that they all have their cell phones out, he scurries into his car, slamming the door closed after him. However, when he tries to start the car, it doesn't.

He tries several times, but only smoke comes out from the bonnet. Rykan chuckles from behind me, leaning down to whisper into my ear, "I might have broken something when I stopped the car."

My eyes widen as they land on the bonnet. The bonnet had completely lifted from where Rykan pushed his hands up against it. Then I smile, turning my head to look up at him. "You did well, Ry."

His eyes flash with surprise, and his lips quirk up slightly, his arm tightening around me. "Thank you, pretty baby."

Warmth encompasses my cheeks at the pet name. I definitely was not expecting that.

"What the hell?" I hear my father yell out, capturing our attention. "You broke my car!"

"Sorry," Rykan says, although the tone in his voice suggests that he's anything but sorry.

"What am I supposed to do now?" he yells out, glaring fiercely at Rykan.

"I think fixing your car should be the last thing on your mind," Rykan says, pointing over my father's shoulder.

My eyes widen when I see a police car driving towards the school.

"I called them," a girl pipes out from in the crowd, sounding quite pleased by what she's done.

"No!" my father rushes out, his eyes wide in panic. The police car drives through the school gates, stopping beside my father's car, and a policeman steps out.

"We got a report about a child abuser," he says, tucking his belt underneath his belly.

"That's him," another student says, pointing at my father.

"No. It's not me," my father rushes out, holding his hands up in defence.

"Who's the victim?" the policeman asks, his eyes scanning the crowd through his sunglasses. I hesitate slightly, pursing my lips as I slowly lift my hand into the air. His eyes meet mine, and he points at my father. "Is he the perpetrator?"

I nod, swallowing uncomfortably under his intense gaze that I feel right through the lens of his sunglasses.

"Do you have any proof of the abuse?" he questions.

"We witnessed everything," a student yells out, and everyone nods in agreement. "He tried to kidnap her."

"Well, we'll have to speak more at the station. Sir, I'll need you to get into the police car," the policeman says, but my father shakes his head, taking a few steps back.

"No! I'm not going anywhere," he yells out.

The policeman sighs, sending a look that says he should've listened when the officer spoke nicely before suddenly flipping my father around roughly and pressing him against the car. He then cuffs my father before dragging him into the police car and shoving him inside, slamming the door closed.

"You'll have to come with me," the policeman says to me. I nod, but just as I'm about to move, Rykan pulls me closer.

"I'll take her with my car," Rykan says and leaves no room for protest as he grabs my hand and pulls me away.

The crowd separates when the two of us walk through. Rykan leads me to a sleek black *Chevy Camaro* that immediately looks too expensive for me to possibly climb into.

When he sees me hesitating, he chuckles. "The car won't bite."

I roll my eyes at his words, carefully opening the door and climbing into the car. My body sinks into the leather seat. This seat feels a lot more comfortable than any car I've ridden in before.

"You like it?" Rykan asks with a chuckle as he sinks into his seat. I nod with an excited smile, my eyes big. He smiles so softly at me, and it startles me. I need some time, or a lot of time, to get used to this, to him. Usually, he's so cold and makes it quite clear that he doesn't care about me, yet now, he saved me from dying, he saved me from my father, and now he's taking care of me by making sure that I don't have to deal with this situation alone. He's so different now, and yet, there's one thing that still tugs at my mind and keeps me awake at night.

He hasn't told me he likes me.

I explicitly told him how I feel about him, and I even went as far as to ask him if he couldn't like me back, but he hasn't responded. I like the way he's being with me right now, but the fact that he may not still feel anything for me and that he's merely being nice to me because he pities me bothers me. I want to ask him how he truly feels, but I'm afraid that it'll ruin the good place we're in now, and the last thing I want is for him to revert to his previous cold and mean self. I don't think I'll be able to handle it.

"What's wrong?" Rykan asks, his eyebrows furrowing in concern about my sudden silence.

"I'm just nervous. That's all," I lie. I'm too scared to tell him the truth. Is this really what my life has come to? I don't particularly like it, but it's not like I have a choice. I can't lose him.

Not now. Not ever.

CHAPTER TWENTY-SEVEN

I'm nervous.

My hands are clammy as we stand in the police station, awaiting a police officer to come and take my statement. Rykan is quick to notice how nervous I am, and he reaches out, pulling my sweaty hands away from one another and wrapping his own around one. "Don't be nervous. You aren't alone. I'm right here."

It's quite amazing how merely hearing his voice can calm me down and erase all the nerves that flutter within me. It must be the bond.

I nod at Rykan, tightening my grip on his hand as my nerves become more apparent. We wait a few minutes before a police officer approaches us with a file in hand.

He places it on his desk and sits down on his chair, flipping it open. "You two may take a seat."

I nod, slowly sinking into one of the seats and pulling Rykan into the one next to me.

"All right. So, tell me everything," the police officer says, leaning forward in his seat.

I look to Rykan with hesitant eyes, and his soften as he squeezes my hand in encouragement, the look telling me that it's okay to speak. So I take a deep breath before starting to talk and tell the police officer everything. He makes notes in the file as I speak, nodding every now and then. The entire time I speak, Rykan's hand remains firmly wrapped around mine, squeezing it in encouragement every time I hesitate a little. By the time I'm done talking, I glance at Rykan briefly, and the way he looks startles me.

He looks so . . . angry. His jaw is clenched, and a certain darkness in his eyes scares me slightly. I've never seen him look like this before, not even when he was so close to beating Jackson up in the cafeteria. Is he getting angry because of what happened to me? Is he getting angry . . . for me?

"Do you have any proof of the abuse?" the police officer questions, and I nod, pulling my cell phone out from my pocket.

"I took some pictures of my wounds and have a few recordings," I say, clicking on the photos and sliding my cell phone to him. "This should be enough, right?"

He scans through all the photos before clicking a recording I took. My father's voice instantly fills my ears. *"I give you everything. I feed you, I send you to school, and I provide a roof over your head, and this is how you repay me? By trying to tattle-tale to the nurse in the emergency unit?"*

I immediately recall when this happened. It was once when he'd beaten me so badly that I had to go to the hospital's emergency unit to get treated, and I nearly told the nurse who took care of me everything. I would have had he not barged in there, shutting me up.

"Clearly, I've been too nice to you lately. Looks like you need a lesson."

"No, please. I'm sorry. I won't say anything, I promise. So, please, don't hurt me." I hear my own pleading voice surface in the recording.

My father laughs at my begging. *"I don't think I want to."*

I flinch at the sounds of slapping, kicking, and hitting filling my ears. Upon seeing my reaction, the officer stops the recording, staring pitifully at me. "This is enough to get him arrested, although you may have to testify against him in court. Is that all right with you?"

I nod, knowing that I don't have any other choice. Suddenly, a growl erupts from beside me, capturing the attention of everyone in the police station. Rykan looks beyond furious now, his free hand clenched into a fist. "How dare he? How dare he lay his hands on *my* mate?"

I won't be surprised if everyone here finds out he's a werewolf.

"I'm going to kill him," he growls. That voice . . . it's Axel. He stands up abruptly, stomping to the cell where my father is.

My eyes widen in alarm, and I quickly get up, rushing after him. "Axel!" I yell out. "Axel, stop."

He wraps his hands around the iron bars of the cell, and fear paints my father's features. "I'm going to kill you."

It's not a threat. It's a promise.

"Axel," I exclaim, grabbing his arm that shakes viciously. "Axel, calm down."

When he turns his head to mine slightly, his eyes are glowing that familiar molten gold colour. I scan to our surroundings before grasping his face between my hands and pulling his head down to mine, whispering, "Axel, calm down."

"I'm going to kill him," he growls, but I shake my head.

"No, you're not," I say, staring at him with firm eyes. "He's going to get punished. I promise he will. So please, don't do anything drastic that will land you in jail."

His golden eyes flash.

"Please," I plead, and almost immediately, the golden glow in his eyes disappears, leaving behind my favourite chocolate browns. I release a breath in relief.

"Lexia," he breathes out. Rykan is back.

"I know. I know," I say. "It's okay. You're okay."

He nods, relief flooding his eyes.

"Is . . . is he okay?" I hear someone hesitantly ask.

I turn to them, nodding. I can only hope I managed to hide his glowing eyes from them in time. "I'm sorry," I say, and he nods in understanding. Judging by the lack of fear on their faces, I can conclude that they didn't see his glowing eyes.

"He . . . he's a werewolf!" my father suddenly exclaims, pointing at Rykan. I turn to him with a fierce glare, shutting him up.

"Don't listen to him," I say to the officers.

"Don't worry. We won't," one assures, chuckling lightly. I nod, thankful. "We'll take care of this, so you may leave now."

I nod, grabbing Rykan's hand and pulling him out of the police station. The moment we're outside, I pull him aside. "Are you okay?"

He nods. "I'm fine now. I just lost control for a moment."

I stare up at him with worried eyes. "Why did you lose control?"

He hesitates, his eyes avoiding mine. "I just . . . I got so angry at him for hurting you so many times. Axel felt it even more than I did. All he wanted to do was torture your father so that he'd feel the same pain you have all these years."

I can't help but smile slightly.

He may not have confessed to me, but this shows that he cares, and for now, that's enough.

CHAPTER TWENTY-EIGHT

"You need to stay with me."

I blink up at him in surprise. We left the station, and now we're sitting in his car, talking about where to go. But I was definitely not expecting him to suggest that I stay with him.

"Stay? As in . . ." I trail off when he nods.

"I want you to live with me."

I choke on air, shaking my head. No, there's no way I can do that. Besides, why is he even suggesting this? No way does he really want me to live with him.

"Listen, I know this is very out of the blue, and you must be so startled, but just hear me out," he rushes out, and I nod. "It's dangerous for you to go home right now. Even though we've kind of gotten rid of one threat, there remains another one. *Jackson.* If you go home, he'll be able to find you easily, and if he gets to you, he really might succeed in killing you this time."

My eyes widen. He's right.

"But I'm staying with Lia right now, so shouldn't that be fine?" I ask, but he shakes his head.

"He'll expect it and will easily be able to obtain her address. My pack . . . we live in the forest, and there's a barrier around us to hide us from people's view. He won't be able to find you there," Rykan says, assuring me.

"But what about your pack members? Don't you remember what happened last time?" I question, recalling how one of them tried to kill me.

"You don't have to worry about them. As long as you bear my mark, they won't touch you," he assures.

I bite my lower lip in hesitance. Can I really do this? Can I really go and stay with Rykan? In a place filled with other werewolves who no doubt hate me just because of the fact that I'm human?

"Look, how about this?" he says. "We try it, and if you don't like it, we'll figure something else out."

That does make me feel a little better, but nevertheless, I'm still hesitant. I've never lived with any man besides my father before. Besides, Rykan and I aren't even in a relationship. I don't even know what kind of relationship we have. We're more than friends, but less than dating. What does that even mean? It's all so confusing, so how can I possibly live with him while having so many unanswered questions?

"Lexia," he softly calls out. "Don't wrack your brain about this. All you have to do is say yes or no."

I understand what he's saying, but I can't go into this blindly. I can say no and risk Jackson showing up at Lia's home, or I can say yes and risk possibly getting murdered by one of his pack members.

I can't say I have any good options. But I guess I have no choice. I'll just have to take the risk.

"Fine," I finally say. "I'll stay with you."

A smile appears on his face almost immediately, and he nods, switching on the car.

I turn away from him, leaning my back against the leather seat as he starts to drive, watching the world as we pass it by. When we reach the forest, I sit up. All I see is trees, so where can the pack be?

Suddenly, Rykan's mark on my neck throbs, catching my attention. Almost immediately, the trees start melting away, disappearing, causing my eyes to widen, and soon I no longer see the forest filled with trees. I see the familiar pack that looks like a village on its own. How?

"It's magic," Rykan says upon seeing my reaction. "We asked a witch to enchant a spell around the pack to keep it hidden from outsiders."

"So how can I see it right now?" I ask.

"Because of my mark," he simply says, driving down a dirt road.

An *ah* escapes my lips. I do recall his mark throbbing about a moment ago before the forest melted away. Werewolves who stand beside the road bow to Rykan as we drive past, and I know why. I remember what they called him the last time I was here. Alpha. Their leader.

But he's so young. How can a mere eighteen-year-old be an Alpha? I don't question it, though. I feel like it's not my place. I don't fail to notice the way they stare at me as we pass them by, their eyes narrowed and inquisitive. Their stares make me uncomfortable.

"Don't worry," Rykan says, reaching over the console to grab my hand. "Like I said before, they won't hurt you."

I nod, swallowing. He soon pulls up to a house that immediately strikes me as familiar. It's the house from before. Rykan parks and switches off the car, turning to me with a slight smile on his face. "Welcome to my home."

He then gets out of the car, and I follow suit, waiting for him to round the car before letting him lead me into the house. It's quite impressive, but not in a fancy way, a built-in fireplace with grey couches and teal-coloured cushions in front of the flat-screen television. When I look further in, it leads to a perfectly sized kitchen with marble décor and silver culinary tools. Then, near the living room, is a wooden staircase that leads to the upstairs.

"Are you hungry?" Rykan asks, walking into the kitchen and pulling open the silver refrigerator. I shake my head. After everything that's happened today, I don't think I can keep anything down. He nods, closing the fridge. "Come on. I'll take you to your room."

He leads me up the stairs to a hallway with doors on both sides. He walks to the end of the hallway and opens the door, revealing a bedroom. It's not as big as his, which I remember from last time, but it has everything I could possibly need with a bed, desk, and window at the end.

"Sorry it looks like this. I wasn't expecting a guest," he says, staring awkwardly at me.

"It's fine. I don't need much anyway," I say with a shrug, walking into the room. The moment I'm fully inside, I notice the familiar duffle bag and school bag placed neatly on the bed.

"I had Cole pick it up from Lia's house for you the moment you agreed to live here. And don't worry about her. He explained everything to her and assured her that you're okay," he explains, and I nod.

"Do you live here alone?" I ask, coming to sit down on the bed.

"Well, I used to live with my sister, but she found her mate and moved into a place of her own, so I guess the answer is yes," he says, staring at the ground.

So he lives here alone, and now I'll be staying with him in this house, alone. Somehow, this feels dangerous. I should've asked him before agreeing. But there's nothing I can do about it now.

"Anyway, you must be exhausted from everything that's happened. You should get some rest. I'll be downstairs if you need anything."

Then he's out the door.

CHAPTER TWENTY-NINE

Rykan

I'm a liar.

But I can't help it. It was the only way to get her to stay with me. The truth is, Jackson isn't on the loose. I got two of my pack members to secretly take Jackson's unconscious body from the school and bring him to the pack's prison, but I didn't tell Lexia that. Instead, I lied and told her that she had to stay with me in order to be safe.

Why did I do that? I honestly have no idea. But the moment we got to the car and I realised that I potentially had to say goodbye to her, I froze up. I didn't want to say goodbye. I didn't want her out of my sight. And I don't know why.

"Rykan," I hear a familiar voice call out, pulling me out of my thoughts.

"Hey, guys," I tiredly greet Cole and Gage as they walk up to me.

"How did things go at the station?" Gage asks.

"Her father was arrested, and he'll have to sit for trial," I say, and he nods. Then I notice the harsh stare Cole's sending my way. "Is there something you have to say to me, Cole?"

"Why did you do that?"

"Do what?"

"Stop the car," he clarifies.

I don't answer.

"Do you have any idea how dangerous that was? Luckily, everyone was too distracted by what was happening to think about the fact that no human could stop the car like that. Otherwise, we would've been in trouble."

I sigh, running my fingers through my hair. "I know."

"You knew? Are you sure? Because if you did, then you should've just stayed still," Cole says.

He's right. I didn't know. I still don't know. I didn't think about any of the potential consequences for my actions. All I could think about when Lia told me everything was that I needed to save Lexia from her father, no matter what it took, and when I saw her in his car, I knew that the moment he drove through those gates, I would never see her again. I couldn't let that happen. So I acted without thinking, and now I'm getting flack for it.

"I don't agree with Cole's manner of speaking, but I do agree with what he means, Rykan," Gage softly cuts in, the look in his eyes is gentle as he stares up at me. "Why did you do that?"

"I . . . I don't know," I admit, looking down.

"Is it because of that Lexia girl?" he softly asks, and when I don't answer immediately, he gets his answer.

"I don't understand you, Rykan," Cole says. "Why would you . . . why would you risk everything for a girl? A girl who's not even your mate?"

"She *is* my mate," I instinctively say, causing surprise to flash in their eyes, as well as through me. Why did I say that?

"You're starting to sound just like Axel," Gage notes. "But I don't understand. Why? This bond isn't supposed to affect you in any way, so why? Why are you acting like this?"

Gage looks truly baffled by why I'm acting the way I am and why I'm doing the things I'm doing. But the truth is, I don't have an answer for him. He's right. The bond between Lexia and me is only supposed to affect her and not me, yet here I am, feeling this strange way for her. I can lie and blame the bond, saying that I have no idea what's happening, but I don't want to because the truth is, it started before I bit her and gave her my mark.

When I caught her running from her father that day and saw how truly scared she was, I felt the strange desire to protect her from him and all harm. That was the start of it. That day—the way she made me feel—it left me breathless. I couldn't and still can't understand why I felt that need, that need to protect her, that need to hold her, that need to touch her, that need to kiss her. It was overwhelming, and it still is.

"Rykan," Gage softly calls out. "Do you . . . do you have feelings for her?"

Do I have feelings for her? My feelings for her . . . they're nothing less than complicated. It's the truth that she makes me feel something, something that I've never felt before, but it's strange. I don't know what it is.

"I don't know," I say.

"Why don't you try explaining to us what you're feeling?" Gage suggests.

I hesitate. Can I really do that? How do I tell them everything without getting judged by them? No, I shouldn't think like this. They're not only my pack members, but they're also my best friends. So I have to trust that no matter what I might say, they won't judge me. So, taking a deep breath, I take the leap.

"When she's around, I can't keep my eyes off her. When she's not around, I find myself unconsciously looking for her. When she smiles or laughs, my chest becomes warm, and I find myself smiling at her. When she's in trouble or in danger, all I want to do is protect her, even if it means I get exposed. When she stares up at me with those eyes, giving me the look that I don't think she realises she gives me, I want nothing more than to kiss her. But she's so innocent and pure that I fear I may taint her if I even come close to her. And she's . . . she's so beautiful. The most beautiful girl I've ever seen. Her beauty ... it's so different to any other girl. It's so true, so raw, so pure. I can barely believe someone like her exists."

They don't say anything, just stare at me with wide eyes and dropped jaws.

"Why ... why aren't you saying anything?" I question, their stares making me uncomfortable.

"Rykan," Gage gasps out. "You like her."

I what? I like her? Who? Lexia? No, there's no way.

I shake my head vehemently. "No, Gage. You're wrong."

"He's not wrong," Cole cuts in, his eyes darkening. "You like that human girl."

Then he storms out of the house. Cole's angry. Even if I deny my feelings, he's convinced, and he hates it. He hates humans even more than I do. Although he hates them because of me, the thought of me having fallen for a human girl makes him angry. I completely understand why he's reacting the way he is, but still. I wish he wouldn't be angry at me.

"I'll fix it," Gage says before following Cole. I release a breath of frustration.

"Alpha," a voice calls out, and I turn around, my eyes landing on one of my pack members. "He's awake."

I nod, walking ahead. I exit my home and walk to the pack prison, and the guards bow to me when I walk in. I take the long staircase down to the cells and walk to one of the interrogation rooms where they inform me, through the mind-link, he's being held.

The guard opens the door for me, and I step inside, my eyes landing on a huddled body in the corner. His ankles and wrists are chained to the wall. I smile at the state he's in. His bare body is covered in slashes and cuts, dry blood staining his skin and fresh blood dripping from his face. When he senses my presence, his head lifts, and his swollen eyes meet mine.

"Well, hello, Jackson."

CHAPTER THIRTY

I miss him.

Rykan . . . how I miss him right now. It's been a few hours since he left me to rest, and I was so mentally exhausted that I fell asleep almost immediately. But now I'm awake, and I have been for the past half hour. I know that he said that I can find him downstairs if I need anything, but I'm feeling a little shy, and God knows why. Probably since it's just the two of us in this house.

So I just remain lying in this bed, avoiding going downstairs, and it's going well until my stomach decides to growl. I rub my stomach with my hand. I didn't have any breakfast or lunch today, so it was only a matter of time before I got hungry. Groaning, I sit up in the bed, and my eyes find the window. It's only now that I realise how much time has passed by. The sun is setting, and orange, pink, and red colours are splattered across the once-blue sky.

Sighing, I lift the covers and get up from the bed, slipping into a pair of fluffy bunny slippers, which I found in my duffle bag. I walk to the door and pull it open slightly, popping my head out through the gap, and peeking out into the hallway. The hallway is empty, luckily, so I exit the room, walking down the hall and slowly descending the stairs. I tip-toe all the way down because I know about werewolves' heightened senses, which means that they can easily hear me coming.

I soon find myself in the kitchen, pulling open the refrigerator and searching for something to eat. There isn't much in there besides bottles of water. However, when I open the freezer compartment of the refrigerator, I spot a packet of frozen vegetables. That, along with a few spices, will be enough to make a vegetable soup for myself. I wasn't planning on cooking, but there doesn't seem to be anything else I can nibble on to satisfy my empty stomach.

I grab the frozen vegetables and, after searching for spices, I place them on the kitchen counter. I'm about to look for a pot when I suddenly hear someone talk behind me. "So you're Lexia."

I jump in my spot, twisting around to face the person. My eyes immediately land on a beautiful girl with long golden-brown hair that cascades over her shoulders and down her back with a pair of chocolate-brown eyes identical to Rykan's, minus the golden specks. Can they possibly be related?

"Who are you?" I find myself asking. She smiles, taking a few steps towards me. I swallow, instantly feeling intimidated as her tall height practically towers over me. Well, that and the fact that she's a werewolf. She can no doubt snap me in half with that strength of hers.

"I'm Alex, Rykan's older sister," she answers. "And you're Lexia, Rykan's mate."

My eyes widen at her words. Sadly, I'm not Rykan's mate.

"I'm not his mate," I say, shaking my head. "I'm human."

"Honey," she says, leaning forward slightly. "You bear his mark, which means that whether you're a werewolf or a human, you're his mate."

I'm . . . I'm his mate? Somehow, I feel like I shouldn't just believe in her words so easily. I mean, how can a werewolf have a human mate? It's unheard of. But I don't say anything to her. I just stay silent.

Then she peers over my shoulder. "What are you making?"

"Vegetable soup," I answer.

"Oh," she says, walking over to the refrigerator and pulling the door open. "Of course Rykan doesn't have any food in his house."

She closes the door and turns back to me. "I apologise for my brother. Ever since I left to live with my mate, he doesn't really keep food around the house."

I nod, pursing my lips.

"If you want, you can come and eat supper at my home. My mate loves food, so I always cook up a feast," she says in offer. Her mate? Another werewolf? I want to play it safe and say no, but my stomach growls before I can say the words. She laughs in response. "Come with me."

She beckons me to follow her before she starts walking, and I do with my short legs struggling to keep up with her long strides. She really is Rykan's sister.

Alex's home is a few houses down from Rykan's. However, hers isn't nearly as big and extravagant as his. It's a nice cottage that's big enough for her and her mate, and maybe even a child in the future. The moment I enter, I'm engulfed by a certain warmth, but it's not physical. It's the aura in the place. It just feels so homely.

"Shaun, I'm home! And I brought a guest!" she yells out, and almost immediately, a figure rushes into the living room. This must be her mate. He has gentle features, his hair the same colour as Alex's and his eyes big and blue.

"Hi. You must be Lexia, Rykan's mate," he says, smiling down at me. I don't protest when he calls me Rykan's mate, although I do wonder why they're all calling me that. *Isn't our bond a fake mate bond and not the real thing?*

"Nice to meet you," I say, shaking his hand.

"She's staying for dinner," Alex says, walking to the kitchen that forms a part of the living room.

"That's great. Ever since Alex told me about you, I've been very excited to get to know you," he says.

They talked about me?

"Come take a seat, Lexia," Alex says, beckoning me over with her hand. I walk to the kitchen and take a seat at the table, Shaun taking one at the head. Alex then starts placing multiple bowls of various foods onto the table, from roast chicken to potato salad. It all looks so good that my mouth can't help but water at the sight.

"Dig in," Shaun says.

I nod, grabbing the plastic spoon and dishing potato salad onto my plate. I then grab myself a drumstick and a garlic roll. The moment I bite into the garlic roll, I hum as the butter melts in my mouth.

"Is it nice?" Alex asks, and I nod, smiling at her.

"So, Lexia, how did you meet Rykan?" Shaun asks, stuffing a potato into his mouth.

I pause my eating, lifting my head to his. "At school. He's in my class," I simply answer.

"He's mean, isn't he?" Alex whispers, and I can't help but nod. She laughs. "He's always been like that. He doesn't let people in easily."

"But has he let you in yet?" Shaun suddenly questions, causing me to freeze. Has he? Has he really, or does he just pity me?

"I . . . I don't know," I honestly answer, my gaze falling onto my food instead of on them. I feel almost embarrassed to admit this, but it's true, and no lie I may tell will change that.

"I'm-I'm sorry for asking," he says with a stutter, staring at me with guilt swirling in his eyes. Awkward silence follows, and it's my fault, but I don't have the energy to fix it.

Suddenly, the front door opens, and someone walks in. I don't even need to look up to know who it is—that familiar vanilla and cinnamon scent invading my nostrils.

"Rykan," Alex exclaims. "Come on. Have some food."

The chair next to mine scrapes against the floor as he pulls it back before sitting down. I don't lift my gaze once, keeping my eyes fixed on the food that hardly seems appetising to me anymore. Rykan doesn't bother acknowledging me, ignoring me as he dishes food onto his plate. I can feel both Alex and Shaun's eyes on me, but I don't dare look up, picking up my fork and stabbing it into a potato. I then proceed to stuff it into my mouth quite unattractively and chew angrily.

What's up with him now? He was so nice earlier, but now he's ignoring me completely. I don't think I could've done something wrong, since all I did since getting here was sleep. Maybe he's just naturally a moody person, but that still doesn't mean that it's okay for him to take it out on me, especially when I've done nothing to deserve it.

Pouting in anger, I stuff potato after potato into my mouth, only stopping once my mouth is completely filled, and I choke slightly. A hand immediately pats my back, and a glass of water appears in front of my face. "Slow down, pretty baby."

The pet name just causes me to choke even more, and the potatoes come falling out of my mouth onto my lap as I cough. The moment my mouth is empty, my cheeks flush in embarrassment at what just happened, and in front of Rykan. I grab the glass before bringing it to my lips and taking long gulps of water. However, the universe must hate me because I end up choking on the water, and it ends up coming out of my mouth, wetting my clothes and the tablecloth.

When I awkwardly look up, I notice them staring at me with surprise in their eyes, as if they can't believe what just happened, and it just makes me more embarrassed.

"You've made a mess, baby." Rykan speaking has my head snapping to his, and when I do, he's already staring at me with furrowed eyebrows. Then, as if to make things worse for me, a burp escapes my mouth, and my eyes widen as my hand flies up to cover it. Rykan's mouth quirks. "You need to calm down."

He grabs a napkin from the table and uses it to clean around my mouth. I pout as he cleans me up, gathering the potatoes from my lap in a napkin and closing it before placing it on the table. He uses another napkin to wipe the stains off my lap.

When he's done, his eyes lift to mine, and when he quickly notices my pout, his thumb comes up to swipe across my lower lip. "Don't pout, pretty baby."

My cheeks flush in embarrassment, and I look away from him. The moment I do, my eyes meet Alex's, and when they do, I immediately notice how she's smiling at the two of us.

"You don't know?" Shaun suddenly pipes out, staring at me with a slight smile. "I'm not so sure about that, because I think I do."

I quickly realise he's talking about Rykan letting me in. When I look back at Rykan, he's no longer looking at me. Instead, his focus is now fully on eating the food on his plate.

"I think you mean a lot more than you think you do," Alex suddenly says, staring at me with a certain softness in her eyes.

I do?

Why don't I believe that?

CHAPTER THIRTY-ONE

The crisp night air bites at my skin.

It's cold as Rykan and I leave Alex's home, making me shiver. I rub my hands up and down my arms in an attempt to warm myself up.

"Are you cold?" Rykan asks, glancing at me. I shake my head, although I'm certain it's quite obvious that I'm freezing right now. Coldness and I have never been friends, considering the fact that I'm pretty much sick all throughout winter, always having some kind of cold or flu. "Don't lie to me."

My head snaps to Rykan at his tone. The way he said it, it's like he was scolding me. Staring up at him with furrowed eyebrows, I question, "What's up with you?"

He merely shrugs in response, not looking at me. I roll my eyes at him, thankful when his home comes into view. I practically run to the front door, basking in the warm air when I walk inside. Now this is what I like. I rush over to the fireplace, holding my hands out close to the fire, allowing the heat of it to encompass them.

"You must have been really cold," Rykan says from behind me. I turn to him with a glare.

"If you knew, you should have given me your jacket or something. I've been in my school uniform all day," I say, tugging at the ends of my skirt.

"Why didn't you change into something more comfortable earlier? I especially had someone pick your things up," he says.

"I was too tired earlier," I say, turning back to the fire. I hear Rykan walk away, but I don't bother to ask him where he's going. I bend down onto my knees in front of the fire. A gush of cold wind comes through the window, causing me to shiver. "Oh, it's cold."

Suddenly, I feel something fluffy being placed over my shoulders, instantly warming me up. A blanket. I tilt my head to the side, surprised to see Rykan on the floor behind me. "What are you doing?"

"What does it look like I'm doing?" he says patronizingly.

"Exactly," I emphasize. "Why?"

He merely shrugs, wrapping the blanket tighter around my body. I welcome the warmth it brings, tugging at the ends of the blanket. Then I look at him, noticing how he's merely wearing a short-sleeve sweater. "Aren't you cold?"

His mouth quirks, almost as if he finds my question amusing. "I'm a werewolf. We don't get cold."

"Ah," I say in understanding. "But then, why do I get cold?"

"Because you're not a full werewolf. You merely possess some of our abilities," he explains, and I nod. "But if you're willing, we can share the blanket. I really don't mind."

I shove him, but he barely moves an inch. He laughs, leaning forward and wrapping his arms around my form from behind. I freeze at the action, my cheeks heating up as he places his chin on the top of my head. This is strange. He's strange.

"You . . . you've been strange lately," I say, unconsciously leaning back into his chest.

"Don't you like it?" he questions, and I'm quick to shout out *no* in fear that he may pull away.

He laughs at me. "I guess I've just finally decided to stop fighting what's between us and embrace it instead."

"And what exactly is between us?" I ask, unable to stop myself even though there's a big chance I won't like what I hear.

"Not sure," he answers. My heart stops. "But it's definitely something more than friendship, and if you're willing, I'd like to explore where this can go."

"I want to, too," I shyly mumble, my gaze fluttering to the floor and the fluffy brown rug. Then I'm reminded of something. "But what do we do? I don't think Cole approves of . . . well . . . whatever this is."

His arms tighten around me, as if he can sense my worry. "It doesn't matter. It's my life, and I make all the decisions. He'll just have to deal with it whether he likes it or not."

"But he's your best friend," I remind him. "I don't want to be the cause of you losing your best friend."

"If he's really my best friend, he won't get between us," he insists.

Although I doubt Cole won't try to convince Rykan that this is wrong, I nod. If Rykan's optimistic about this, then I should be, too. Cole's his best friend, after all, not mine, so he should know him best.

I close my eyes, leaning my back further into him, loving the warmth from his body radiating onto me and wrapping around me like a thick blanket. Then he says something that has my eyes snapping open in surprise.

"Sleep with me tonight."

I twist around in my spot, staring up at him, stunned. He looks completely serious, no aspect of amusement anywhere on his face. "Me . . . sleep with you?"

He nods. "We aren't going to do anything. We'll just be sleeping."

Somehow, I feel like the moment I climb into the same bed as him, that's going to change.

"I . . . I don't know," I mumble, looking down. He places his finger under my chin, tilting my head upwards so that our eyes meet.

"Once again, you're thinking too deeply into this," he says, staring pointedly at me. "Why don't you just let go for once? Don't think and just do what you want to. Can you do that for me? Huh, pretty baby?"

I swallow, allowing myself to relax. Staring hesitantly up at him, I let him reach up to caress my cheek ever so gently.

"What do you want, baby?" he murmurs, his voice husky.

"I want to sleep with you," I find myself admitting. My desire for him consumes me to the point that I'm no longer shy about admitting my need for him.

He smiles, his arms instantly coming underneath me before picking me up bridal style. The blanket falls into a puddle on the floor, and I wrap my arms around his neck, snuggling into him as I seek to find the warmth I lost. He carries me all the way up the stairs to his bedroom, kicking the door closed behind us before taking me to his bed and setting me onto the covers ever so gently. I can hardly believe that this man is being so gentle with me. I didn't think he was even capable of being gentle.

Rykan climbs onto the bed, his body hovering over mine as he uses his hands to keep his weight off me. His eyes are dark as they stare down into mine, the golden specks becoming more apparent and shining more brightly than ever before. He leans down, and his nose grazes over my neck. Then he inhales sharply, lifting his head to look at me.

"I can smell it," he murmurs. "Your desire."

He can even smell my desire for him?

"You want me," he states, and I shamelessly nod, the desire for him to touch me much greater than any shyness or embarrassment. He smiles, appearing pleased by this. Then he leans down again, his lips meeting mine softly.

A sound of pleasure escapes my lips as I wrap my arms around him, wanting him even closer. Without warning, his tongue dives into my mouth, causing my back to arch against the bed. I wrap my legs around him, pulling him closer to me until our sensitive flesh touches, causing me to gasp at the foreign yet pleasureful sensation.

He rips his lips away from mine, focusing on my neck instead as he litters it with kisses before placing one last kiss on his mark. "Mine," he murmurs. "All mine."

Then he pulls away completely, his hands landing on my thighs and holding them there firmly. He leans down again, placing a painstakingly quick kiss to my lips before pulling away again.

"I want it off," he says, a guttural sound erupting from the back of his throat. He tugs at my skirt, and without thinking, I lift my hips to allow him to remove it, which he does, slowly sliding the thin material down my legs and tossing it somewhere.

The cold breeze brushes my bare skin, and I shiver. I instinctively pull my legs up, but Rykan is quick to grab them, pinning them down with his hands. I reach up with my hands, my fingers tugging at the hem of his sweater. He understands because he quickly pulls the sweater over his head, revealing his toned chest to me.

And there it is. That tattoo. I sit up slightly, tracing my fingers over it, admiring the beautiful art. He grabs my chin, tilting my head to the side, and then his fingers land on my own tattoo, a pleased smile tugging at his lips.

Then he kisses me, his tongue diving into my mouth in a way that has my back arching into him. This kiss? It's nothing like the previous one. This one is passionate, animalistic, and claiming. I delve my hands into his hair, tugging at the silken strands.

He lays me down again, his lips not leaving mine as he reaches down to unbutton my shirt with his skilled fingers. Soon, all the buttons are loose, and I can't help but lift myself slightly so that he can pull the shirt off my body. That leaves me only in my underwear and bra underneath him, meaning that he can see almost everything, as well as every single flaw.

As if sensing the sudden change in me, he pulls back and caresses my cheek. "So beautiful."

My cheeks flush at the compliment, my eyes fluttering closed as he lays kisses down my body. "Absolutely beautiful."

His mouth goes further and further down until it reaches the band of my underwear. This is it. The moment it's off, there's no going back. This is really happening. I'm going to lose my virginity to Rykan. There's no turning back now.

"Don't worry, pretty baby," he suddenly murmurs against the material of my underwear, his eyes set on mine. "You'll be able to keep your purity tonight."

My word, that was the hottest thing I've ever heard. I must have lost my mind.

Suddenly, he rips my underwear off me, tossing the shredded pieces aside. He chuckles at my surprise. "But that doesn't mean I can't treat my baby right."

I gasp when a finger gently slides into my burning heat. I squirm in discomfort. He moves his body up, placing soft kisses on my neck as I get accustomed to the strange feeling. But the moment his finger begins to move, the discomfort fades away and is replaced by a rush of pleasure that consumes me almost immediately.

Reaching up, I grip his shoulders with my fingers, my face scrunched up in pleasure. Rykan's tongue touches my ear. "Tell me how much you love it."

"Don't stop," I choke out, and he listens, sliding another finger into me. "Please don't stop."

I should be embarrassed by the way I'm begging for him, but I can hardly think about that right now, even though I'm certain this will come to haunt me in the morning.

His pace quickens, his fingers working against me in a way that has me quivering, and soon something foreign builds up in the pit of my stomach.

"Let go, pretty baby."

The mere sound of him calling me by that pet name has me letting go, a wave of pleasure crashing over me as I come apart underneath him. Pulling his fingers out, Rykan plops down beside me. He pulls me against him, smiling lazily at me. I can't help but smile, too, through my tiredness. He truly looks happy, and that makes me happy, too. There's nothing I love more than seeing him be happy, I'm certain.

I should regret what we just did, considering the fact that I barely know him, but I don't. Instead, I'm happy about it and if this was so good, I can't even begin to imagine what it will be like when he fully unleashes himself upon me.

I can't wait.

CHAPTER THIRTY-TWO

I'm in the forest.

Trees surround me, and the wind is blowing through my hair. This feels quite strange because it almost feels like I'm in a dream.

"Amaris," a voice whispers, echoing through the area. "It's time for you to wake up."

Wake up? Wake up from what? This dream?

"Where are you? Who are you?" I yell out, looking around me.

"I'm inside you," the voice responds.

Inside me? What's that supposed to mean?

"Amaris, the time is near."

"What time?" I yell out.

"Time for us to awaken in the world," the voice answers. Awaken in the world?

"But until then, stay with Rykan. Don't let him go for anyone."

"What about his mate?" I question, as it suddenly comes to my mind.

"We are his mate."

Then I wake up. I'm in Rykan's bedroom, encased in his arms as he sleeps peacefully next to me. I sigh, leaning back into the bed. What in the world was that?

"Pretty baby," Rykan suddenly murmurs, grabbing my attention. I twist over so that I can face him, my eyes fixed on him as he sleeps. "So pretty."

I can't help but smile. Is he . . . dreaming about me right now? I reach out, caressing his face softly with my fingers. This man, how's he even real? He looks so beautiful, even when he sleeps, with his long eyelashes fanning his face. I envy him a little. Why couldn't I have been born with half of the beauty he has? I think then I would've had many boyfriends under my belt. But now, as I look at him, I realise why things are the way they are. If I'd had multiple boyfriends already, I probably wouldn't still have my purity, and I wouldn't have been able to give him any special part of me. So I'm glad because if there's one person I want to give my everything to, it's him. It's all him.

He snuggles closer into me, his face coming to bury itself in my neck, and I fight the urge to laugh when he unconsciously sniffs my neck before placing a soft kiss at the base. He's so precious, and I'm glad that I'm able to see this part of him. I guess even the coldest and meanest people have their own soft side, and I'm lucky to see his.

I can't even believe that there was a time he hated me, especially with the way he treats me now. Now, he treats me like someone precious and important to him, and it's more than I could ever have asked for.

"Pretty baby," he murmurs against my sensitive skin, sending a shudder through my body. "You're mine. All mine."

I read that werewolves are quite possessive creatures, and I guess it's true. I recall him calling me his last night, too. The mere thought of last night and what we did has me blushing. I'm thankful that he's asleep and can't see and tease me about it. I can still hardly believe what we did and how shameless I was in expressing my need for him. I even begged him not to stop. I can only hope he doesn't wake up and decide to tease me about it.

"I'm yours," I whisper to his sleeping form, and it's true. Last night confirmed everything. I'm his, irrevocably and undeniably all his. A sound escapes his lips, and it surprises me. Did he just . . . purr?

His arms tighten around me, and he snuggles his face deeper into my neck. He's surprisingly a heavy cuddler. I never would've guessed. Not that I'm complaining. I've never cuddled with anyone before, and I'm finding that I quite like it.

Suddenly, the door opens, and Gage walks in, startling me. "Rykan—"

Both our eyes widen in shock, and I quickly use my hands to try and push Rykan away from me, the key word being try, because he's too strong for me, and he just ends up pulling me closer, groaning lightly. "Stop, pretty baby."

His arms tighten around me as he pulls me against him, sighing in contentment afterwards.

"Well, this is quite the surprise," Gage notes, staring at the two of us with amusement swirling in his eyes.

"It's-it's not what it looks like," I rush out, shaking my head.

"Oh, I think it's exactly what it looks like," he says, peering over me to look at Rykan. Then he gasps, his eyes widening. "Oh my! Are you naked under there? Did you two have sex?"

"No!" I rush out with wide eyes.

"But you did something," he says, and the smile on his face surprises me. Doesn't he hate me with Rykan just like Cole does? If he does, then why does he look so . . . pleased?

"Is there something you need?" I ask in an attempt to change the subject.

"Oh, it's time to leave for school," he informs. "I thought he would be awake and ready by now, like he usually is. I guess he must've had such a good night's sleep that he's sleeping in."

"Oh my." I gasp, my eyes widening. "What time is it?"

He smiles in amusement. "It's time to get up."

"But I can't," I whisper. He merely smiles, flashing a mischievous wink my way before walking out, shutting the door behind him. I sigh in frustration, tapping Rykan on the arm. "Rykan, it's time to get up."

"Not now," he says, groaning.

"Yes, now," I say, insisting while trying to pry his arms off me but failing miserably. "If we don't get up now, we'll be late for class."

"Who cares?" He groans out, frustration evident in his voice.

"I care!" I yell, frowning down at him. Suddenly, he's sitting up, glaring down at me.

"You're annoying," he says, my frown deepening at his words. But then he leans down, his lips meeting mine briefly. "But I like you, so it's okay."

Then he's up from the bed and inside the en-suite bathroom. I sit there, touching my lips in disbelief at what just happened.

Did he just confess to me?

CHAPTER THIRTY-THREE

"Lexi!"

"Lia!"

We both run to one another, crashing into each other's arms quite dramatically.

"I missed you so much." Lia sniffles into my shoulder, and I nod, hugging her tighter.

"Me, too." I sniffle.

"Are you okay?" Lia questions when we pull away. "Cole told me everything, but I was still so worried about you."

"I'm okay. Rykan helped me a lot," I say, and she nods, smoothing her hand over my hair.

"I'm glad." She breathes out and then hugs me again. I don't know how long we keep standing there, just hugging, only pulling away when students, some I know and others I've never seen, approach us.

"Lexia."

"Are you okay?"

"What happened to your father?"

"Do we need to testify about what we saw?"

I'm instantly overwhelmed by the number of questions and attention. No one has ever paid this much attention to me before. Lia immediately notices, stepping in front of me. "Listen, Lexi's okay. Her father is in jail, and we'll let you know if any of you need to testify. Now please leave. She's been through a lot, and you're overwhelming her."

Luckily, they all look pretty sympathetic toward me and just nod before all walking away and disappearing down the hall.

I release a breath of relief, turning to Lia. "Thank you."

"Of course," she says, flashing me a thumbs up. "Let's get to class."

She hooks her arm around mine, and we walk to the classroom. The moment we're inside the class, I notice the pile of red envelopes, roses, and chocolates on a desk at the back of the class, specifically, Rykan's desk. Is it Valentine's Day or something? But even if it is, every student is afraid of Rykan and what he may be, so why would they be giving him roses and chocolates?

"What's going on there?" I ask Lia, pointing to Rykan's desk.

"Oh, things changed quite a lot in that one day," she says.

"Like what?" I question.

"Well, instead of being enemy number one, Rykan has now become desirable number one," she informs.

"Why?" I question, my eyebrows furrowing in confusion.

"Because he helped you," she states. "Almost half the school saw what happened yesterday and found it so nice of Rykan to help you in your predicament. So everyone's now on his side, and girls are finally appreciating him for the fine specimen he is."

What? Everyone likes him now, especially the girls? A foreign feeling builds up in me at the news, and I can't help but frown in dissatisfaction.

"What? Are you jealous now that girls are going after your man?" Lia teases, smiling mischievously at me. I shake my head with a pout. She laughs. "You are. Admit it."

"Fine! I'm jealous!" I admit with a huff. "But wouldn't you be if you were in my situation? I mean, the girls in this school are so pretty. I can't possibly compete with them."

"What are you talking about?" Lia suddenly yells out, startling me slightly. "You're really cute, Lexi, and you have your own charms. Any guy would be lucky to have you."

"Really?" I ask, my voice small and soft.

She nods vehemently. "Of course!" she exclaims. "You have no idea how cute you are."

"Well, I was born this way," I say in a sassy tone, flipping my hair over my shoulder. Within moments, the two of us burst into laughter.

"And what's so funny, girls?" a voice suddenly says from behind us, startling us into jumping in our spots.

"Gage," Lia breathes out as we turn to the two boys behind us. "What are you doing here?"

"If I'm not mistaken, this is my class," he teases, smiling cheekily at her.

This is quite odd, because either Gage is just a really nice person, or there's something between the two of them. However, considering how serious they seem to be about the whole mate thing, I doubt it. "Anyway, back to what you guys were laughing about . . ."

Lia places her palm underneath my chin, saying, "Isn't she so cute?"

"Why is that funny?" Gage questions, staring at us with inquisitive eyes. Lia moves her hands away, sending an unimpressed look Gage's way.

"It's not," she says before turning around and walking to her desk.

My eyes land on Cole, who wordlessly stands there, his hands tucked into his pants pockets, and I raise my hand up to him. "Hi."

He scoffs before stomping away with a roll of his eyes. I purse my lips at his attitude, dropping my hand back to my side. Gage leans in closer, whispering into my ear, "Don't worry. I didn't tell him about this morning."

If he's like this with me without knowing what Rykan and I did, then I don't want him to ever know, because he may kill me if he finds out. Leaning in closer to Gage, I whisper, "He's really against werewolves going out with those who aren't their mates, huh?"

Gage casts me a hesitant look. "It's . . . it's not necessarily that. He's been with other girls before who aren't his mate."

"Then why is he so against me?" I question. Gage doesn't answer. "What? Did I do something wrong? Is it because I . . . you know . . . called you guys dogs on the first day?"

His head snaps to mine. "I thought you said you didn't say anything."

My eyes widen. Cole helped me that day, luckily, and now I've messed it up. "Never mind that. Tell me why Cole hates me so much."

"It's . . . it's because you're . . . human," he hesitantly says.

"Because I'm human?" I repeat, my eyebrows furrowing in confusion. "What does that have to do with anything?"

"Cole hates humans."

"Why?"

"That's . . . personal," he says, looking uncomfortable with what I've asked. He's not going to tell me anything, I quickly realise.

"Fine. Don't tell me anything." I huff, sighing through my nose.

"Look, it's not like that —" He starts, but I stop him by lifting my hand in the air.

"It's fine. He's your best friend, and because he doesn't like me, I can't force you to spill his secrets to me," I say in defeat, and he nods, looking thankful that I've stopped asking him questions on this topic. He then proceeds to walk to his seat, but not without sending a disgusted glance at the pile on Rykan's desk, causing me to laugh.

"And who's making you laugh like that?" a familiar voice questions as an arm slings across my shoulders. I tilt my head up, smiling when my eyes meet Rykan's. However, the smile quickly fades and turns into a frown when I smell him. He quickly notices. "What's wrong?"

"You smell like girls," I say, scrunching my nose up in distaste.

"They ambushed me at the entrance. I barely got away," he says defensively.

"You're a strong, pure-blooded Alpha. I'm sure getting away from a few girls is no problem for you," I say, staring pointedly at him. His mouth quirks, and he leans down slightly.

"Aw, is someone jealous?" he muses, a mischievous glint in his eyes.

I huff, turning my head away from his. "Me? Jealous? Don't flatter yourself, Rykan, whatever your last name is," I say.

"It's Rykan Amano, and I truly think you're jealous," he says. I roll my eyes at him. "Why? Does the thought of other girls touching me bother you?"

Yes, it does bother me, but I'll never admit that to him. As if it's the universe's way of punishing me, images fill my mind of many girls swarming around Rykan, touching him with their dirty fingers, and some even going as far as to kiss him on the cheek, leaving behind a lip print. The mere thought has my hands clenching into fists at my sides.

They probably did do that earlier. They probably touched him with those sinful hands that have probably touched so many other boys before. Here I am, with my purity still intact, and Rykan being the only man to have ever touched me.

Then I remember that I'm not the only one who's had the pleasure to touch him, to be with him. He's been with other girls, who knows how many, who have touched him before me, who got the privilege to pleasure him in a way I haven't yet.

The mere thought makes me angry, and suddenly, I

imagine choking faceless figures with my bare hands, wanting to erase them from existence so that I might be the only one, and that thought scares me. Why am I even thinking like this?

"Your possessive side is coming out. The need to claim our mate as ours, finally," the voice in my mind says.

"The need to claim him as mine? What does that even mean?"

"Pretty baby, are you okay?" I hear Rykan ask me, but I ignore him, focusing on what the voice in my head told me. Claim him as mine . . . do I want that? How can I even do that?

"We need to keep other she-wolves away from our mate. You have to keep them away," the voice says.

"Other she-wolves? Female werewolves?"

"Baby . . ." I hear Rykan call out, but once again, I ignore him.

The voice is right. If I want to keep Rykan as mine forever, I need to keep other girls away from him, werewolves and humans alike. Now I'm determined. I'm not letting Rykan go.

Not ever.

CHAPTER THIRTY-FOUR

"Come at me."

I hesitate. Rykan and I stand opposite one another on the pack's training grounds. He's decided to train me in my new abilities, and that includes fighting. However, now that he asks me to attack him, I hesitate. How do I even do that? Do I just launch myself at him?

"What's wrong?" Rykan asks, pulling me out of my thoughts.

"I have no idea what to do," I admit, staring helplessly at him.

"Just do what feels right," he says, beckoning me to come forward.

Releasing a breath, pushing all hesitation out of my mind, I run to him with my eyes closing in fear when I reach him and crash into him. He catches me, his hands gripping my hips. My eyes hesitantly open, and I look up at him with a scrunched face in awkwardness. That didn't go well.

He chuckles in amusement. "What were you trying to do?"

I shrug, pursing my lips in embarrassment. What a way to impress the person I like.

"Should I pair you up with a pack member instead? Will that ease your nerves?" he asks, staring down at me with raised eyebrows. I shake my head. Who knows what that pack member may do to me? Rykan still has mercy on me, but that pack member won't. "Well then, what do you want to do?"

I shrug once more. He sighs, and I pout. I didn't mean to make him frustrated. "I'm sorry," I mumble, my voice little.

His eyebrows furrow. "Why are you sorry?"

"I'm no good at this," I mumble, staring at his chest instead of his face.

"Baby," he softly calls out. "Baby, look at me."

I hesitantly lift my gaze to his.

"You don't have to be sorry. This is all new to you, so I understand. We can do this at your pace," he assures, squeezing my hips. I nod, although the sorriness didn't leave me. He then leans down, placing a soft kiss on my forehead. "I'm not mad, pretty baby."

He knows. I don't know how, but he knows. He knows that I think he's mad at me.

A small smile tugs at my lips. He's so attentive, and I've noticed.

"Alpha," a voice calls out, breaking our moment. Rykan sighs.

"What is it?" he questions, frustration seeping into his voice at this pack member for ruining our moment.

"We have a visitor," the pack member says.

"Who is it?" Rykan asks.

"Laura."

Rykan's entire body tenses against mine, causing me to look up at him with furrowed brows. What's with this reaction?

Then a woman approaches us, and my breath hitches when I lay my eyes on her.

She's so beautiful, with long blonde hair flowing down her back and her eyes a crystal blue colour. She's also so tall, her slender legs going on for miles and her bust straining against the tight crop top she wears. Then she lifts her hand, smiling flirtatiously at Rykan.

"Well, hello, Rykan."

The look in Rykan's eyes as he stares at her lets me know there's something there. Something that I can't figure out. He

looks almost like he's seeing his lover after a long time.
Oh no.
Who is this woman?

CHAPTER THIRTY-FIVE

Laura.
My eyes are fixed on her as I peek into Rykan's office through the little opening of the door. It feels wrong of me to spy on the two of them, but I can hardly stop myself. Whoever this woman is, she was important to Rykan once, I can tell, especially from the way he looks at her. The mere sight has my heart clenching painfully in my chest, but I ignore the feeling. Right now, I need to focus on what's going on here.

"Don't let her near him," the voice in my head suddenly whispers. *"She's trying to steal our mate from us."*

"Do you know her?" I whisper, knowing how sensitive werewolf ears are, and if I just speak a little too loud, Rykan will know that I'm here, and I don't want that.

"No, but I can sense her intentions," the voice says, a bite to it. *"I can also smell her desire for him. The two of them, they've slept together before."*

I flinch at the voice's words. So she's one of them. One of the women who have been with Rykan. The revelation makes me annoyed, and a certain bitterness floods under my tongue.

"What are you doing here, Laura?" Rykan speaks, pulling me out of my thoughts and capturing all my attention.

"Can't I visit an old lover of mine?" she says patronisingly, staring up at him with pouty lips. "I miss you."

Rykan scoffs. "Really? That's surprising considering the fact that you broke up with me."

She broke up with him? Who would ever break up with Rykan?

"You know that I had no choice," she says, her voice softening. "I met my mate and had to leave with him. You know that I would never have left you if I had a choice."

Why does hearing her talk like this to him hurt so much? No, I know why. It's because if she hadn't met her mate, they would probably still be together, meaning that he wouldn't have looked twice at me. It won't surprise me if she's still in his heart.

"Don't think like that," the voice says. *"We are the only ones in his heart."*

"Whatever," Rykan says, looking away from her. "Why are you even here? What about your mate?"

She freezes, and he quickly notices.

"What's wrong?" he asks, the underlying concern in his voice causing me to wince, almost as if I'm in pain. I am.

"He . . . he died," she says, and he flinches. "He was poisoned with silver by humans, and he died."

"I . . . I don't know what to say," he mumbles, staring pitifully at her.

"But that doesn't matter," she says, her mood suddenly lightening. "It hurt only for a little while because of our mate bond, but I didn't love him. Not like I loved you. Not like I still love you."

Rykan doesn't respond.

"Rykan," she calls out, taking a step closer to him. "I don't know about you, but I see this as the Moon Goddess's way of bringing the two of us together again."

"Bullshit," the voice in my head says.

"Now that my mate is gone, we can be together again," she says, taking his hand into hers. He doesn't argue with her nor pull away from her. Why isn't he doing anything? Does he not even think of me in this moment?

"Laura—"

She shushes him by placing her perfectly manicured finger on his lips. "Don't. Just give in, Rykan. Just be with me."

When she leans in to kiss him, my eyes widen in fear, but I'm quickly spun around and pulled into an unfamiliar chest.

My heart stops, but just as I'm about to pull away, the person speaks. "Don't look."

Cole. Why did he grab me? Why is he holding me? I thought he hated me.

However, that hardly matters as sadness seeps into my body. Tears come spilling from my eyes and stream down my face. I press my face firmly into his chest as I cry, the tears unstoppable.

Then the sadness transforms into something else. Something uglier. Anger.

I clench my hands into fists at my sides. How dare they? How dare *he*? I thought we had something special. I thought he liked me. But I guess it's not enough. I guess his feelings for his ex are much greater than his feelings for me.

My body starts to shake in anger. Rykan . . . *I'm going to hurt him.*

"*No,*" the voice is quick to exclaim. "*Don't get angry. Don't be angry at Rykan.*"

"*He hurt me.*"

"*I know, but don't let your anger consume you. It's not time yet. You have to wait,*" the voice rushes out.

"*Wait for what?*"

"*I'm not ready yet,*" the voice rushes out. "*If you force me to come out, we'll get hurt. We have to wait.*"

"Wait for what?" I roar, my voice no doubt catching the attention of everyone who's nearby.

"*Mating,*" the voice says, the desperation apparent. "*We have to wait for mating. We need his energy.*"

"Mating?" I laugh.

"What's happening?" I hear Rykan question.

"There's no way I'm mating with him," I say, my voice deadly.

Then I storm away.

CHAPTER THIRTY-SIX

Blood.

That's all I can see.

I'm not in control. Something, no, someone else is in control, and whoever it is, they can't seem to control their actions either. We're filled with rage, and we're consumed by it.

"Lexia!" I can hear someone call out, but I don't stop, my fingers clawing at flesh. "Lexia!"

Arms wrap around me, and I freeze.

"It's okay," the person rushes out. "It's okay, baby."

The control the person has on me slips, and slowly, I can feel myself being able to move my limbs at will again. I slump into the person's hold, that familiar vanilla and cinnamon scent invading my nostrils. My head lifts, and my eyes widen when they meet Rykan's. The amount of shock and concern in his eyes . . . it's so overwhelming.

"Rykan," I whisper, my voice weak. "Something's wrong."

"I know, baby," he softly says, pulling me against him. "It's okay. We'll figure it out. Together."

Then everything becomes dark.

CHAPTER THIRTY-SEVEN

Rykan

Lexia is a werewolf.

I don't know how or why, but she is. I saw it. Yesterday, my ex-girlfriend, whom I broke up with a couple of months ago, showed up, claiming that her mate is dead and that we can be together again. Like a complete fool, I let myself be under her spell for a brief moment, but by the time I snapped out of it, it was too late. My pretty baby had already seen and heard everything and thought that I was probably going to leave her for Laura. She's wrong. I would never do that, especially when she means so much to me, but she doesn't seem to know that, so she got so angry and stormed out of my home.

As soon as she ran outside, she started attacking my pack members left, right, and centre, ending their lives with one quick strike to their throats. The moment I encased her in my arms and looked into her eyes, I knew that it wasn't my baby in control. Something, no, someone else was in control, the obvious pointer being her eyes, her eyes that glowed a bright silvery colour.

Then she passed out in my arms. I brought her to the pack hospital where she was immediately hooked up with an IV and a string of medicines, half of which I've never seen in my life. Whatever took control of her, although I think that it was her wolf, has now let go of the reins, and Lexia is back. However, she won't wake up.

It's been three days since then, and she still hasn't opened her eyes once. And although I'm extremely worried about her, there's one thing that constantly tugs at my mind. If she's really a werewolf, why didn't I realise it from the beginning? How was she able to hide it from everyone? From me? No, she didn't hide it. Judging from how helpless and scared she looked when I held her in my arms, she had no idea of what she is, and that doesn't make sense.

Also, her father's human, and I'm assuming her mother was, too. So how? Up until she had that outburst, she smelled like a human, and now afterwards, she smells like a human again. It was just for a brief moment that she smelled like one of us. I've never seen anything like this before, and if I'm being honest, it scares me. There can really be something wrong with my baby.

"Rykan," Gage calls out, pulling me out of my thoughts, and I turn to him.

"Did you find something?" I ask, hoping that he's at least found something that can be the cause of this, but when he defeatedly shakes his head, the glimmer of hope seeps out from my body.

"I really have no idea what's going on with Lexia, and because you told me not to tell any other pack members, I can't ask them if they may know," he says with a sigh, but it had to be done.

With how my pack members treated her when she first came here, I don't want to take any chances. Besides, I don't need more drama right now. I have enough on my plate with an unconscious mate and a pestering ex-girlfriend.

"All right. Thanks," I defeatedly mutter before walking back to Lexia's hospital room, a room private from the other wards as I ordered.

When Gage and I arrive in the waiting area just outside her room, I'm surprised to see Cole standing at her door, peering in through the window. The truth is, ever since what happened, Cole hasn't left the hospital except to shower or eat something. Otherwise, he always lingers close by her room, and I have no idea why. Is he just watching over her for me while I figure things out?

"Is he still here?" I hear Gage mumble from behind me, and I nod.

"He hasn't left since the incident happened," I say before walking over to where Cole stands. I tap him on the shoulder when I reach him, and the concern and worry swirling in his eyes when he turns to me shocks me. What is up with him?

"What are you still doing here? You should go and get some rest."

He surprises me by shaking his head. My eyebrows furrow in confusion. Along with the concern and worry, fatigue is evident in his eyes with the black bags underneath them apparent. He looks exhausted, yet he refuses to leave here, and I have no idea why.

"Rykan's right, Cole," Gage says, coming to stand next to me. "You should leave and get some shut-eye. You look terrible."

"Will everyone just stop telling me to leave?" Cole suddenly says, startling Gage and me. "I'll go if I feel the need to, so stop forcing me."

He then turns back to the window. Gage and I share a confused glance at one another. Why is he acting like this? Is there something that I don't know?

"Cole—"

"Alpha," a voice calls out, cutting me off. Although I'm annoyed, when I see that it's the doctor, I rein it in. "She's awake."

Cole's the first one to rush into the room before even I can, but I don't question it.

My focus fixes on Lexia, who's awakened for the first time

in three days. I rush into the room, freezing in the doorway when I see Cole standing over my mate, holding her fragile hand in between his own. My eyes widen at the tears that spill from his eyes. What the hell does he think he's doing?

"Cole, where's Rykan?" my baby asks, her voice so weak that it tugs at my heartstrings. I rush over to her bedside, pushing Cole out of the way and grabbing her hand instead.

"I'm right here, pretty baby," I say, staring down at her with a gentle gaze. She releases a breath of relief.

"I'm right here with you, and I'm not going anywhere. I promise."

"I'm angry at you. You have a lot of explaining to do," she says, doing her best to glare at me, and I can't help but smile at the cute little pout on her lips. I feel like kissing it away, but I stop myself. Now's probably not the right time.

"Yes. I'll explain everything," I assure her, nodding. I touch my free hand to her cheek, and her eyes flutter closed as she leans into my touch. All I do is stare down at her, unbelievably happy that she's finally awake and that she looks somewhat okay. But then I feel the anger radiating from behind me, and when I turn around, my eyes meet Cole's dark ones. There's definitely something going on here.

I turn back to Lexia and mutter, "Pretty baby, I have to go and deal with something quickly, but I'll be back before you know it."

"Promise?" she mumbles, her voice childlike, and I nod.

With one swift kiss to her soft skin, I leave the room after sending Cole a look to follow me. When we're far enough from the room for anyone to hear us, I stop, turning back to Cole.

"What the hell's going on with you?" I say, glaring down at him.

"I have no idea what you're talking about," he lies, his eyes avoiding mine.

I scoff, folding my arms across my chest. "Bullshit. Don't lie to me," I grit out.

He doesn't respond.

Realising that there's no other way to get him to fess up, I use my Alpha voice as I command, "Tell me the truth. What do you want with my mate?"

"She's not your mate!" he yells out, his eyes burning with anger as he stares at me, but there's something else in there, too. Jealousy. "What you two have is not a real mate bond. It can't be."

"And why can't it be?" I challenge.

"Because I knew!" he exclaims. "I knew that there was something special about her from the beginning and that she was something supernatural."

"And how did you know that?" I question. He doesn't answer immediately, infuriating me even more. "How?"

"Because she's my mate."

CHAPTER THIRTY-EIGHT

Where's Rykan?

He promised that he'd be back soon, but it's been hours since he left, and he still hasn't returned.

"He must be held up somewhere," Gage says, excusing him, but I don't buy it. Why do I feel like this has something to do with his ex? Is he with her again? "I'll go find him."

Gage is quick to be out the door, the sound of it slamming in his haste causing me to flinch in surprise. I don't know how long I just remain lying in the hospital. The only time I sit up is when my cell phone starts ringing on the bedside table. I reach over to grab it, wincing at the slight sting in my head before answering the call.

"Where the hell are you?" Lia says, well, more like yells into the call. "It's been three days since I've seen or heard from you. Three days! What the hell, Lexia Leigh?"

She's using my full name. That means that she's angry, very angry.

"Lia, calm down," I say.

"Don't tell me to calm down," she says. "Where the hell have you been?"

"I . . . I was sick. Terrible flu," I awkwardly lie, hoping that she can't hear it through my voice. "I was passed out all throughout the three days. Barely got up to eat."

"Oh my God," she says, gasping and worry seeping into her voice. "Are you okay?"

"Yeah. I'm much better now," I say, and she sighs in relief.

"I'm so glad. I thought those werewolves hurt you or

something," she says.

"No. Rykan would never let them . . ." I trail off, the smile slipping from my face. Is he really with that Laura girl? But I just woke up. That jerk. "Look, I have to go. I just took my medication, and it makes me really sleepy. We'll talk again tomorrow." And I hang up before she gets a chance to speak or possibly protest about how this was such a short call.

With a groan, I get up from the bed, pausing when I realise that the voice is quiet now. It didn't talk much in the first place, but suddenly, it feels like it's missing, like I'm missing something.

"Hey," I call out. "Are you there?"

No answer. I try again. And again. But there's no answer. Maybe it's just ignoring me on purpose, as per usual.

Shrugging it off, I leave the room, looking down the hall and releasing a breath of relief when it's empty. I tip-toe down the hall so as to not alert any nurses who may be doing their rounds. Just as I'm about to leave through the ward sliding doors, a beep resonates in my ears. I pause, my eyebrows furrowing as I turn around in my spot. Where's that sound coming from? I walk back down the hall, stopping at the private room at the end, right next to mine. I stand by the window, peering inside through the glass. My eyes widen at what I see.

A woman. She lies lifelessly in the hospital bed, her limbs unmoving at her sides, and patches that lead to multiple IV drips litter her arms. A mask is over her face, which she breathes into, and the machine she's hooked up to is beeping furiously.

Suddenly, nurses come rushing past me, a few bumping into me in the process of getting to the door and inside the room. They all gather around the bed, hiding the woman's body from me. I stand up on my tip-toes to try and see over them. One nurse climbs over her body and starts doing CPR on the woman while the others check her IV's and adjust the settings on the machine.

The nurse doing CPR instructs the other nurses to give her things that I've never heard of until today, and within moments, one of them hands her a sack with a transparent liquid inside, and she rips off one of the patches before pumping it into the IV. The other nurses line up other sacks with a variety of coloured liquid inside onto the IV, pumping the foreign fluid into her body.

Suddenly, a hand grabs my arm, and I'm spun around, my eyes widening when they meet Gage's. "Come with me."

He then proceeds to drag me back down the hall and out of the ward.

"Wait," I exclaim, pulling back against his grasp, causing him to stop and turn to me with frustrated eyes. "What's going on, Gage? Who was that woman?"

"That's none of your business," he's quick to say, his tone of voice causing me to flinch slightly. "Now come with me."

He then drags me out of the hospital and to a building I haven't seen before today. Where's he taking me? He opens the door and pushes me inside, shushing me when I open my mouth to speak. He then leads me up a stairs and to a door at the end of a hall. He knocks once on the door, and when we hear a gruff come in, he lets go of me and walks away without a word.

I'm left with no other option but to go inside the room, which I do, shutting the door gently behind me. The moment I'm inside, I'm hit with that familiar scent of vanilla and cinnamon.

"Lexia?" I hear Rykan call out, and confusion is laced in his voice. I ignore him for now, my eyes darting to the contents of the room. It immediately strikes me as an office, bookshelves pushed up against both opposite walls with two dark brown coloured couches and a low-cut rectangular coffee table in the middle, and in the centre at the end of the office sits

Rykan at a shiny wooden table with a stack of paperwork in front of him. "What are you doing here?"

"Where were you?" I question instead of answering his question, staring at him with narrowed eyes. "You said you would return soon, but you still haven't, and I was forced to come to you myself."

"I got caught up with work. Sorry," he half-heartedly apologises, and I can't help but scoff.

"That's really all you have to say?" I exclaim in disbelief. "I was unconscious for three whole days, and none of you knew if I would actually survive, yet the moment I wake up, you leave me to do . . . work? What the hell? I almost died. Do you not even care about me?"

"It's not like that—"

"Then what the hell is it like?" I cut in. "Because right now, it feels like you don't care about me."

He opens his mouth to say something, but he quickly shuts it, deciding against it. I stare impatiently at him, glaring at him as best I can. He better give me an excellent explanation, or I'll remain as angry as I am.

Suddenly, he's up from his seat and right in front of me, the suddenness making me flinch in surprise. His hands grasp my face, and he stares down at me, his eyes holding something they never have before. Vulnerability.

Reaching up, I brush a strand of hair out of his face. "Are you okay?"

"No," he admits, surprising me. "I'm far from okay."

"Why? What's wrong?" I gently ask, my voice softening from earlier. He shakes his head, grabbing my hand on his face with his own.

"I don't want to talk about that right now," he says.

"Then when?" I ask.

"Tomorrow," he promises. "But tonight, I don't want to think or talk about it. I just want to be with you tonight. You trust me, right?"

One would think that what happened between the two of us before I passed out would make me a little wary around him, but surprisingly, it doesn't. Instead, I still trust him. I think it's mainly because I know that he'll never break my heart, and that's why, no matter what happens, I trust him.

"I trust you," I say with a nod of my head.

He smiles, although his smile doesn't reach his eyes. I want to ask him more questions, but I refrain, not pushing him away when he leans down to kiss me. The moment his lips touch mine, relief washes over me. Even in my unconscious state, I missed him, his touch, and his lips. However, there's something different yet familiar in the way he kisses me, his body pressing into mine in a way that almost has me over-whelmed.

He rips away from me almost immediately, his stare heavy and filled with something else. Lust. And the next words he utters have me weak in the knees.

"I want to mate with you."

CHAPTER THIRTY-NINE

Rykan doesn't wait another second after hearing my yes before he whisks me away to his home.

The moment we're in his bedroom, I'm pulled against Rykan's hard body and his lips instantly find mine. I allow myself to relish the kiss I've missed so much, even in my unconscious state. I dig my fingers into his thick strands of hair. When he deepens the kiss, I don't hesitate to kiss him back with as much vigour as him.

I know that there's still a lot to address, but right now, all I can focus on is him. His touch, his smell, his kiss. Everything else can be dealt with later.

Rykan dips his head, kissing along my jawline and down to my neck and collarbone. I grip his shoulders when he bites down on my skin, causing my eyes to flutter closed at the sensation. Then his lips trail up again to his mark.

I gasp when he bites into the mark, and pleasure floods my body. It almost feels like he's marking me all over again, just better and less painful the second time around.

"Rykan," I murmur, gripping his shoulders with my fingers.

"Yes, pretty baby?"

"It-it feels so good," I stammer, hardly embarrassed about my admission.

I feel him smile against me before he sucks on my sensitive skin over where he bit, as if he's healing it. Pulling his head back up, I meet my lips with his, tugging him even closer until there's absolutely no space between us. I can feel everything, even the hardness of his muscles flexing underneath my fingertips. I can't help but smile into the kiss, pleased that I have this effect on him, too.

Rykan's not shy in his exploration of my body, his untamed hands roaming all over me, my waist, hips, and back. Anticipation flutters at my skin where his fingers touch, anticipation of what's to come.

Leaning down, he grabs the underside of my thighs and picks me up, my legs automatically coming to wrap around his waist, causing my lower region to press against his. With a gasp, my head tilts back. Rykan kisses wherever he can as he backs me into the wall.

"Let me take you to bed," he murmurs as I tangle my fingers in his hair. I nod, allowing him to carry me to his bed and set me ever so gently onto the mattress after pulling back the sheets for who knows what reason.

"Why did you get rid of the sheets?" I ask against his lips.

He leans down, his body hovering over mine as he murmurs, "We don't need those for what we're about to do."

I giggle while tugging at the hem of his shirt, which he doesn't hesitate to drag off his body and toss aside, mine joining his shortly after. I only have a moment to admire his perfectly sculpted chest before he grasps my face between his hands and kisses me again.

I'm not sure how the rest of my clothes come off my body in between the endless kisses that Rykan presses to my lips and my skin. I'm shivering slightly when the breeze brushes my bare skin. Unlike before when I still had my underwear on, now I'm completely naked, and he can see everything.

"You're beautiful," he murmurs, dipping his head to place a kiss between the valley of my breasts. "So beautiful."

He rises up, his fingers gripping my inner thighs as he comes to situate himself perfectly at the centre of me. He smirks down at me, the laziness in his eyes making me smile.

He looks so relaxed, unlike any other time, and I want to savour this moment forever.

"You have no idea how long I've spent wanting you like this," he admits, surprising me. Up until a short while ago, I was convinced he hated me, and yet now, he sits between my legs with his lips on my bare skin. How things have changed.

"I want you," I admit. My body is burning with desire for him, and I can't wait another moment to have him completely. He presses his hand harder against me as a result of my words, and a gasp escapes me at the foreign yet pleasure-filled feeling.

Finally, his fingers touch the most sensitive part of me, and a sigh of relief escapes.

He leans down, murmuring into my ear, "You're soaking wet for me, baby."

My cheeks flush at his words, heat creeping down my neck and travelling to the rest of my body. I waste no time in getting rid of the rest of Rykan's clothes, literally tearing the material off his body in my haste. I'm not shy in running my fingers along his bare skin, almost as if it's the last and only chance I may ever get. There's an insatiable fire inside me, a fire that won't be put out until I have all of him.

Suddenly my legs are around his waist, and he uses his one hand to pin both of mine above my head and keep them there. With his free hand, he grips my chin in his hold, forcing me to keep my eyes locked with his. Judging by the devious glint in his eyes, he's enjoying this. Really enjoying this.

"You're mine," he murmurs into my ear, and with one single movement, he's inside me. "Forever."

I can hardly breathe for a long moment. All I can manage is a small gasp. Everything, all at once, makes sense to me. It's at this very moment that I feel something change between us and in me. It's almost as if I've been charged with a certain power that's almost as strong as the pleasure Rykan gives me.

Even in the white ceiling, I can see it.

My silver glowing eyes.

However, I can hardly pay attention to it, especially as Rykan starts to move his hips. He lets go of my hands, and I immediately grip his shoulders, my fingernails digging into his skin. This is it. This is what I've been craving all along, ever since I met him.

It's like something has exploded inside me, something so overwhelming that I nearly come undone right away.

"You feel amazing," Rykan praises into my ear, his fingers digging into my hair and pulling as he moves, causing the feelings of pleasure to ricochet inside me. I pull his lips back to mine, kissing him deeply. This urges him to move faster, igniting my body alight with pleasure. I can't get enough of him.

The string of moans tumbling out of my mouth blends in with the rushed breaths and soft groans that escape Rykan as his tongue comes diving into my mouth, moving as frantically and fast-paced as his hips.

"You're mine," he growls once more, as if he's saying a mantra.

"I'm yours," I say as I breathe out, and my eyes shut in pleasure. "All yours, Rykan."

He growls at the sound of his name leaving my lips, and after that, his name is the only thing that leaves my lips as his pace increases even more. Vivid colours blind my vision as my eyes roll to the back of my head.

The feeling of him moving inside me and hearing him whisper toe-curling phrases into my ear tips me over the edge all too quickly, and with a loud gasp, I come undone under him. Rykan follows soon after me, his hands gripping my body desperately. With one last kiss, Rykan draws away from me, plopping onto the bed next to me. I watch him, his dark hair flattened against his head and his bare chest glistening in the moonlight.

He looks over at me, his lips quirking up slightly. This is it. I'm his forever. And he's mine.

CHAPTER FORTY

I*'m happy.*

For the first time in so long, I feel happy, and it's all thanks to Rykan. When I first met him, I never imagined that he would become such an important person in my life, such an important person to me, but he is, and I wouldn't trade it for the world. He makes me happy, and I can never ask for more.

"What are you thinking about?" Rykan softly murmurs, his lips on my skin as he strokes my head.

"Just how happy I am," I admit, snuggling deeper into his hold. I feel his smile against my skin, and he places a soft kiss there.

"I'm glad," he says. "All I want is for you to be happy."

"Now, are you ready to tell me what was wrong earlier?" I question, and he tenses against me. He really doesn't want to talk about it, and although I want to respect his wishes, I think that I deserve to know, especially when he just left me at the hospital like that.

"I—" He hesitates, breaking off briefly before continuing. "I found out something, something I now regret asking for."

"What did you find out?" I ask, trailing my fingers across his bare chest.

"It's not important," he says dismissively, making me frown.

"It must be important if it made you that upset," I protest, sitting up in his arms, causing the covers to fall to my hips. I try not to visibly react when his eyes not so subtly travel to my bare chest before back up to my eyes.

"It's really not something you have to worry about," he says, his hands moving to my hips. "You trust me, right?"

Why does he keep asking me if I trust him? I thought I made myself clear before. I mean, I even gave myself to him despite the concerns that I have.

"I trust you, but you're keeping things from me, and that bothers me," I admit, a frown creasing my forehead.

"I know, baby. It's just . . . it's complicated," he admits, caressing my bare skin with his fingers.

"Are you ever going to tell me?" I ask, and when his eyes lower, I get my answer. Sighing in frustration, I throw the covers off my body, shivering slightly as the cold air caresses my bare skin before moving to get off the bed, but I don't get far before Rykan pulls me back.

"Please don't be angry, pretty baby," he murmurs, intertwining our fingers.

"You're hiding things for me, Rykan. How can I not be angry?" I question in frustration.

He sighs. "Baby," he starts, slowly pulling me back into him. "What do you think about Cole?"

"Why are you suddenly asking me about Cole? What does you hiding things from me have to do with him?" I question.

"Just answer the question," he insists, dismissing my questions.

Sighing in defeat, I say, "What do I think about Cole? I don't know. He's a werewolf, your best friend, and he hates me."

"What do you think of him as a man?" he questions.

"I don't see him as a man. I mean, it's not like he's ever given me the chance to look at him as someone other than your best friend who highly dislikes me," I say with a roll of my eyes.

"And if he wasn't so cold to you? What would you think of him then?" he persists, making me sigh and shout out whatever comes to mind.

"I don't know, okay! Maybe if he wasn't so cold and mean to me, then we'd be friends," I say with a shrug. "Rykan, seriously. What's with all these questions about Cole? Does what you found out have to do with him?"

"No!" he exclaims with wide eyes, sitting up in the process. "I was just . . . wondering."

"Rykan," I call out softly, his eyes snapping to mine. "Do you like me?"

He chuckles, a certain awkwardness apparent in his voice. "Why are you suddenly asking me that?"

"Because I already told you that I like you, and you might've said it once, but now it's starting to really feel like you said it on a whim, and it really bothers me," I admit. Rykan's gaze softens, his hand reaching up to caress my cheek.

"Baby," he gently calls out. "I . . . I have strong feelings for you. I do."

"But then what about Laura?" I question, looking up at him. "I saw everything between the two of you. Do you love her?"

"No!" he exclaims. "I never loved Laura. I've never loved any woman romantically, I swear. You have nothing to worry about, pretty baby."

"But she wants you back," I mumble.

"Well, that's too bad for her then, because I want to be with you," he says, a small smile tugging at his lips as he stares down at me. I nod, relief washing over me. I was worried over nothing. Then his hands travel down to my hips, gripping me gently. "What about you? Do you have any ex-boyfriends I have to worry about?"

I smile, shaking my head. "You're my first and only."

A satisfied smile appears on his face before he leans forward and touches his lips to mine.

"I want to have you again," he murmurs against my lips, pulling me flush against him. I giggle in response, pushing him back until his back hits the bed and his head on the pillow, straddling his waist. He stares up at me with desire swirling in his eyes, his eyes that aren't shy in gazing over every inch of my naked body that's on display for him only.

"Make him ours again," the voice in my head encourages. However, just as I'm about to slide onto him, the bedroom door bursts open, and Rykan instinctively pulls me into his chest. His eyes are wide in alarm, and I desperately clutch the covers in between my fingers in an attempt to hide my bare body from the intruders.

"Who the hell are you?" he yells out as three figures come walking into the bedroom. The woman in the middle chuckles, sunglasses perched high on her nose even though it's nighttime.

"Alpha Amano," she greets, bowing to him, causing his eyebrows to furrow slightly. Then when she takes her sunglasses off, revealing her blood-red eyes, his eyes widen.

"Helen," he gasps, his eyes wide. "What are you doing here in the middle of the night? And what's with the guards?"

"I apologise for startling you, Alpha, but I have urgent business with your mate," she informs, her eyes fluttering to mine. Rykan instinctively pulls me closer to him, his grip on me tightening.

"And what business may that be?" he questions, his voice low.

"If you will, I'll explain everything on our way," she says.

"On our way where?" I ask, speaking for the first time since they got here.

"To our headquarters," she simply says.

"And who exactly are you guys?" I ask, pressing myself against Rykan underneath the three pairs of scrutinizing eyes.

"Well, since you're new to this, I'll try not to be offended," she says, placing her hands behind her back. "We three belong to the Werewolf Council, a group of powerful werewolves who take care of supernatural matters, and I'm Helen Thorne, the one in charge of the council."

"But then, what do you want with me? I'm human," I say.

She smiles, although I can see that it's forced. "I'll give you three minutes to make yourself presentable, and then we'll leave."

Without another word, she and the two men leave the room, closing the door behind them. I look at Rykan with worried eyes. "Rykan, what's going on? What do they want with me?"

"Let's just go with them for now," he says, sitting up. "I know Helen. If it wasn't important, she wouldn't have come here."

He lifts me off his lap and gets up, reaching down to pick up his discarded items of clothing. I do the same, slipping into my pair of leggings, sneakers, and hoodie. But just as he moves to grab his cell phone and keys, I grab his hand, pulling him to me.

"Rykan, they won't hurt me, will they?"

"Baby," he gently says, his hands cupping my face. "Nothing bad will happen to you. I won't let them lay a finger on you."

I nod, allowing him to pull me into his arms. However, our moment is broken all too soon by the bedroom door opening and Helen walking in. "It's time to go."

Rykan nods, placing a reassuring kiss on my head before grabbing my hand and pulling me with him as Helen leads us away and out of the house to a sleek black *Mercedes*. Helen and one of the men take the front seats while the other man squeezes into the back seat with Rykan and me. Rykan frowns at the man, grabbing my hips and suddenly pulling me onto his lap, causing me to yelp in surprise. He pulls me into him protectively when Helen glances at us through the rearview mirror.

Then a cell phone starts ringing. Helen brings the cell phone to her ear, her eyes fluttering to mine briefly as the person on the other side of the call speaks. She hums now and then, nodding her head even though the person can't see her.

"Yes, we have her with us," she says.

Rykan's arms tighten around me, a light growl of warning escaping his lips.

Frowning, I bury my face into his neck, inhaling his scent to calm me. Helen smiles through the mirror, making me uncomfortable.

"Finally, in our custody, we have the Divine Child."

CHAPTER FORTY-ONE

I have no idea where we are.

The car windows are tinted. However, not only can no one see inside from the outside, I can't see the outside either. All I see is black. The fact that the outside of the car is hidden from us doesn't seem to bother Rykan, who seems more focused on glaring at the man sitting next to us. I have no idea why, though. Thus far, the man's done nothing to deserve Rykan's fierce glaring.

Suddenly the car comes to an abrupt stop, and if it wasn't for Rykan's iron grip on me, I would've been sent flying to the front of the car. It doesn't appear to bother anyone else in the car, though.

Helen glances at us in the rearview mirror. "We're here."

She and the two men then proceed to get out of the car, Rykan's arms not leaving me as he reaches down to open the car door, nor when we get out. My eyes widen when they take in our surroundings, especially the huge castle-like building before us. I can barely count the number of floors it must have on my fingers. The building is so tall that it looks like it can touch the sky and heavens alike. The entire building is built of bricks with ancient-style windows and doors that look like they've been there for centuries yet, miraculously, are still in good condition. However the windows are only on the lower floors, but as I look higher up, they disappear.

"Welcome to the Werewolf Council Headquarters," Helen says, gesturing to the building with open arms. "Follow me."

I grip Rykan's hand tightly as we follow Helen through

huge double wooden doors into the building. The building looks old inside, yet quite well-kept, with formal décor. When we walk in, there's a huge room that sort of looks like a ballroom of a kind with a long spiral staircase in the centre. I look around for an elevator or escalator but don't find any. Don't tell me these people walk up hundreds of flights every day.

"All consultations are done on the first floor, and that's where my primary office is. Follow me," Helen says before walking down the room to a long hallway. On each side are doors that I'm assuming lead to other offices. We walk to the very end of the hallway and stop at the last door. Helen pushes it open and leads us inside. The office is quite menial, only consisting of a couch, desk, and chair, and behind the desk is a window that gives off the view of a forest.

Where are we?

"Where are we?" I ask as Rykan pulls me down onto the couch. Helen pulls her chair to face us, and the sound of scraping against the tiles causes me to cringe in discomfort. She sits down but doesn't remove her sunglasses, and I'm grateful for that. I saw her blood-red eyes earlier, and the mere thought of them has me flinching, striking me as familiar, and I have no idea why.

"The location of the headquarters is confidential," she says, her voice clipped.

"I assume you brought us here because you know what Lexia is," Rykan says, raising an eyebrow at Helen. What's he talking about? "I heard what you said in the car earlier. What is the Divine Child?"

"As you might have already concluded after seeing her eyes, she's no ordinary werewolf," Helen says.

"Wait. I'm a werewolf?" I cut in, not understanding what they're saying and why they're calling me a werewolf. I'm human.

"Lexia, there's something you don't know. It's part of what

I've been keeping from you," he says, causing me to frown at him. "But I only kept it from you because I wasn't sure what you are. I wanted to figure it out first before telling you."

"He's telling the truth." Helen cuts in. Rykan nods in agreement.

"So . . . I'm not . . . human?" I slowly ask, and both of them nodding in response. "But how?"

"I'll explain in due time. But for now, we have more pressing matters to discuss," she says, and I nod, leaning forward in my seat. "You two mated."

Almost immediately, like a chain reaction, heat consumes my face at the mention of Rykan and me having had sex. How does she even know that? No, stupid me. We were naked when she walked in on us.

"You two mating is what I and so many others at this organisation have been waiting for," Helen suddenly confesses, her words startling me.

"Excuse me?" I blurt out. They've been waiting for Rykan and me to have sex?

"Why?" Rykan questions.

"Because Amaris's werewolf abilities have been dormant all her life, and mating with you and getting marked by you awakened her werewolf side," she says.

"I don't understand," I say.

"Pure-blooded werewolves have many special abilities that distinguish them from regular werewolves. One of them is the way Rykan first saved you when he marked you. Another way is marking an individual with dormant abilities like you would your true mate, in a claiming way, and by mating with them," she explains.

"Why has her werewolf side been dormant?" Rykan questions.

"Her mother used her powers to make it so. Camouflaging Amaris as a human was the best way she could protect her," she says.

"My mother?" I softly ask, and she nods. "Do you know my mom?"

"Who doesn't know your mother? How can we not when she gave us all life?" she says, a smile coming to her face.

"What's that supposed to mean?" I question, and her smile widens.

"Have you still not figured it out?" she asks, her eyes fluttering to Rykan's. I turn my head to look at Rykan, and almost immediately, his eyes widen, flashing with realisation. "Now you know."

"What's she talking about?" I ask Rykan, but he doesn't answer, staring forward in bewilderment.

"Amaris, dear," Helen calls out, my head snapping to hers. "I know that you think your mother's dead, but she's not. Who died was not your real mother. Your real mother lives."

What's that supposed to mean? Who's my real mother, and why is the person I thought to be my mother not the one who gave birth to me? This is all so confusing.

"Baby," Rykan softly calls out, my head snapping back to his. "Your mother . . . she . . . she's . . ."

He can't seem to get the words out, and Helen sighs.

"Amaris, your mother is the Moon Goddess."

CHAPTER FORTY-TWO

M y mother is the Moon Goddess. The creator of all were-wolves. No way.

I shake my head in denial, scoffing at Helen. "I don't believe you. How's that even possible?"

"Lexia, it's true," Rykan says, causing me to frown. "Just think about it."

"You seriously believe this woman?" I question in disbelief.

"There's a secret that we, as the Werewolf Council, swore to keep," Helen pipes out, capturing my attention. "Thousands of years ago, the Moon Goddess fell in love with a pure-blooded werewolf, and thanks to her foolishness, she birthed a child of her own. Amaris was her name. But the Moon Goddess had many enemies, ghouls who hated her for creating werewolves, supernatural creatures superior to them. Ghouls may be seen as petty cannibals, but they're much stronger than you think. The moment Amaris would awaken as a werewolf, the ghouls would come for her and try to kill her as an act of revenge against the Moon Goddess. So she made Amaris's werewolf side dormant, but soon, when Amaris was of age, she fell in love with a pure-blooded werewolf, just like her mother, and when he marked her and they mated, her werewolf side was awakened. Then the ghouls came for her."

"What happened to her?" Rykan questions.

"She died, sadly, having been murdered ruthlessly by ghouls. But as the daughter of the Moon Goddess, she, just like her mother, had eternal life. And she was born again, the cycle starting over again."

"What happened to her then?" I can't help but ask, curiosity creeping in.

"She died. The ghouls killed her," Helen answers, her blunt answer causing me to flinch. "Unfortunately, as the daughter of the Moon Goddess, that was her fate. Live as a human, fall in love with a pure-blooded werewolf, her werewolf side awakening, and then dying. That cycle repeated countless times from the moment she was first born."

Amaris . . . that name . . . it immediately strikes me as familiar. How can it not, when it's the name the voice in my head has been calling me all my life? Then it hits me like a slap across the face.

"Amaris . . . she's me," I mutter.

Helen nods in agreement. "And just like every time before, your fate has repeated itself once again, today," she says, and I realise that she's right. I've lived my life as a human, met Rykan, a pure-blood werewolf, fell in love with him, mated with him and possibly had my werewolf side awakened.

"Are . . . are the ghouls coming after me now?" I softly ask, fear creeping into my body, and almost as if it's an instinct of his, Rykan's grip on me tightens when Helen nods.

"No. I won't let them lay a finger on her. I'll kill them all before they can." Rykan growls.

Helen shakes her head. "Many pure bloods failed in protecting her so many times before. You won't be any different."

"No," he says, growling and glaring at her. "You're wrong. I can save her, and I will."

She sighs through her nose. "Fine. Do what you want, but while you're thinking of how you can save her, I have a practical solution that can be implemented immediately."

"What is it?" I ask.

"You'll stay here for a period of six months. During your stay, we'll train you both in basic werewolf abilities and your special abilities that come along with being the Moon Goddess's daughter," she says. "With this special training, you'll hopefully be able to survive in the fight against the ghouls."

"Have you tried this before, with my previous selves?" I ask, my heart dropping to my stomach when she hesitantly nods.

"But it's the best chance you've got," she insists. "You won't get training like this anywhere else. Yes, it may not have worked in the past, but it still remains the best chance you have to survive in this fight. As the Moon Goddess's daughter, you were born to fight for yourself. You have never depended on anyone else, not even a pure-blood to save you, and you shouldn't start now. Before anyone else, the only person who can save you is yourself."

What she says makes as much sense as it scares me. I have to fight alone for my own survival? That sounds grim and frightening.

Turning to Rykan, I whisper, "What do you think?"

"As much as I want to tell you that you don't need this and that I'll protect you, I can't deny the fact that this will help you," he admits. "If what she's saying is right and the ghouls are coming for you, you need to be able to protect yourself."

I know what he's saying. He's telling me to do it. I know I can always count on him to be sensible. However, I have to admit, a part of me wants Rykan to protest and just take me home. But I know that's not possible, at least not right now, especially when I have a whole species coming after me.

Taking a deep breath, I turn back to Helen.

"I'll do it."

CHAPTER FORTY-THREE

"How are you feeling?"

I shrug, leaning back into him. It's been a few minutes now since Helen has left Rykan and me alone in her office to organise things for my upcoming six months here. The only thing Rykan has done so far is hold me in his arms and stroke my hair and skin in an attempt to comfort me and calm me. However, unlike any other time when it worked perfectly, my anxiety about what's to come is so strong that it doesn't work, and that scares me even more because if Rykan, my mate, can't comfort me, no one can.

"Don't worry, pretty baby," he says, placing his chin on my head as I come to rest my face on his shoulder. "Everything will be okay."

"How do you know?" I find myself asking because, somehow, I can't bring myself to believe that.

"Because you're not alone," he murmurs, his arms tightening around me. "You have your friend Lia, and your classmates seem pretty supportive of you."

"And I have you," I murmur in contentment, and almost immediately, he becomes quiet, his body tensing beneath mine. My eyebrows furrow. Why has he suddenly gone quiet? Don't I have him by my side, too? I mean, there's no reason for him not to be by my side, especially now that I'm a werewolf. If anything, now's the best time to be together than any other. I can't wait to tell Cole. He hates humans, but now that I'm no longer human, hopefully, he'll accept me as Rykan's mate.

"Lexia," Rykan suddenly calls out.

Calling me by my name instead of by his usual pet name forces me to sit up, frowning at the sadness in his voice.

"No, you're Amaris now."

"I'll always be Lexia," I say, and it's true. I've lived my entire life as Lexia, and if people suddenly start calling me Amaris, it'll feel strange. For now, just until I fully accept what I am and who I am, I wish to remain Lexia.

"Lexia, we have to talk," he says.

"About what?" I ask.

"Us," he says, staring at me with hesitance swirling in his eyes.

"What about us?" I question, as fear of what he may say creeps in. No, I'm just being silly. He cares for me. He likes me. So there's no way he'll ever —

"We should end things between us."

I freeze. *What? What did he just say?*

I think that I heard him wrong, but when I look at him and examine the serious expression on his face, I realise that I heard right. He's ending things between us.

"Why?" I squeak out in shock. "We're mates. Don't werewolves stay with their mates forever?"

"They do," he confirms.

"Then why?" I question.

"Because I've decided to stop seeing other people until I meet my mate," he simply answers.

"But I'm your mate," I mumble, my eyebrows furrowing.

"Yes, because of the mark you bear, you're my mate. But you're not my real mate."

"What's that even supposed to mean?" I question, pulling away from him and putting some space between us.

"It's like you thought before. Our bond isn't real. It's fake," he bluntly says, causing me to flinch. Tears prick at my eyes at his words. Why is he suddenly being so brutal?

"I . . . I don't understand," I mumble, my gaze falling to my lap. "I thought you liked me."

He doesn't respond, remaining silent. What is this? Does he not like me anymore?

"I've decided that this is for the best," he says.

"The best?" I scoff. "For who? Us, or just you?"

"You have a mate out there now, too. You should try and find him," he says.

"I don't want to find him! I don't want him!" I exclaim, my voice softening. "I want you."

He doesn't respond.

"Don't you want me?" I ask in a small voice, a tear escaping my eye. His gaze rises and meets mine, his eyes widening at the tears that fall from my eyes. I could be imagining it, but for a moment, he looks almost regretful before he places a blank mask back onto his face. "Don't you like me anymore?"

He doesn't answer. No, he can't. Maybe there's still hope after all.

I scoot closer to him and grab his hand. "Rykan, what you're worrying about doesn't matter. As long as we still have feelings for one another, we can make it work, and whatever challenges we may face, we'll get through it together."

He looks conflicted, his eyes unable to stay on mine.

"Rykan," I softly call out. "Ry, look at me."

Slowly and very hesitantly, his eyes lift and meet mine again, and the sadness and vulnerability swirling in them makes my heart clench uncomfortably in my chest as I real-ise—he does still want this, me.

Warmth blooms in my chest at the sight of him. He has al-ways had this wall around him, around his heart, keeping me from seeing in, but now, for the first time, he's let his wall crumble to the ground, and he's allowing me to see every part of him. The rawness of it claws at my heart. Then I realise what I'm feeling is hitting me right in the chest where I feel the most.

I can hardly stop the words from tumbling past my lips.

"I love you, Rykan."

He freezes, his eyes widening. I purse my lips, staring hesitantly at him. What he may say to my confession determines what's going to happen. What's going to become of us. If he feels the same way, I would be so happy, but if he rejects me again, I don't think I'll be able to recover from this heartbreak.

"Oh, baby," he says, his hands cupping my face. "I love you, too, baby."

The biggest smile blooms on my face, and I can't help but lean forward, allowing him to wrap himself around me. This is it. This is what I want from the bottom of my heart. It's him. Only him. Whatever may come, can come. Because I know as long as I have him by my side, I can get through all of it.

I'm certain.

CHAPTER FORTY-FOUR

Rykan

She loves me.

My baby loves me. When she confessed to me, it was like all the air was knocked out of my lungs. I was stunned beyond belief, and in that moment, I completely forgot why I wanted to end things with her in the first place. Maybe I'm being selfish, but God. I love her, too. I love her so much that I can hardly believe it.

When I first met her, yes, I thought she was absolutely breathtaking, but I never imagined that she would become such an important part of my life, such an important person to me. I could never have predicted that, in merely a few months, I would love her as much as I do.

But lord, she has all of me. She's encompassed every single part of my heart. There isn't a single part of me that isn't completely filled with her. When she's around, I can't see anything or anyone but her. When she's away, I can't think about anything or anyone but her. When she messages me, perhaps a simple hello with that blushing face emoticon she loves so much, the biggest smile appears on my face, and I'm aware that I probably look like a complete idiot, but when it comes to her, I don't care.

But through all this happiness of us confessing our love for one another, I'm sad, too, because I've just arrived at the pack after saying goodbye to her. That goodbye . . . it was the hardest thing I have ever had to do, especially since I know that I won't see her for six months. I hope time goes by quickly so that I can see my pretty baby again.

"And where the hell were you?" That's first thing I hear when I step inside my home, and immediately, the smile slips off my face when I see who's asked the question. Cole.

"Rykan, where's Lexia? Is she okay?" Gage asks, concern swirling in his eyes. After leaving Lexia at the headquarters, I mind-linked Gage and told him everything, and even though I knew that he would tell Cole, I wasn't anticipating this much hostility from him.

"No, her name isn't Lexia anymore," Cole cuts in. "It's Amaris."

I hate the way he talks about her, the way he says her name. He sounds possessive, like she's an object that belongs to him. It makes my skin crawl.

"So, Rykan, where's my mate?" Cole questions, him calling her his mate causes me to flinch, like I was just attacked. Axel growls from inside me.

"She's our mate."

I want to say the same to Cole, but it will only cause more tension and anger, so I refrain.

"Mate? What are you talking about?" Gage asks Cole.

"Ask him," Cole simply says, nodding his head my way. Gage turns to me with questioning eyes, and I sigh. Why must he put me on the spot like this? This completely ruins my mood.

"He's right," I force myself to say, practically spitting the words out like fire. "Lexia, no, Amaris, is his real mate."

Gage's eyes widen. "Wait, what? Since when?"

"Since always," Cole answers. "She's always been mine, but since everyone thought she was human, I kept it to myself. But now I'm ready to admit to it, and when she's in the same room as me, she'll feel it, too."

Dammit. I forgot about that. Now that her werewolf side has been awoken, she'll feel the mate bond between them.

Will that make her fall out of love with me? I feel almost self-ish for thinking about myself and my feelings at this point.

"So . . . what happens now?" Gage hesitantly asks, his eyes moving between Cole and me.

"Now I'll tell her who we are to one another, and we'll be together," Cole answers, as if my and her feelings for one another mean nothing.

"Rykan, are you okay with that?" Gage asks, his eyes swirling with sympathy as he stares up at me. I want to shake my head and tell them that we love one another, but the words won't come out.

"Now, if you'll excuse me. I'm going to see my mate now," Cole says and is out the door before I can even think of protesting. Biting my lower lip, I run my fingers through my hair in defeat.

I'm so weak.

EPILOGUE

"Cole, what are you doing here?"

I'm confused. Why's Cole here? I thought Helen said that no visitors are allowed, so what's he doing here?

"I've come to tell you something," he says, walking up to me. I furrow my eyebrows in confusion.

"What is it?" I question when he stops right in front of me.

"Do you feel it?" he softly asks.

I'm about to ask him what he's talking about, but I feel it. Something strange. It's almost as if I've been put in a trance, a trance that's causing me to gravitate towards Cole, and before I even realise it, I'm in his arms.

My eyes immediately widen in shock. *What's happening to me?*

"I knew you would feel it," Cole murmurs. "Our mate bond."

"Mate bond? What mate bond?"

"You have no idea how long I've been waiting to call you my mate," he says, causing me to freeze.

"Call me his mate?" His words have me breaking out of whatever trance had overtaken me, and I immediately pull away from him, pushing at his chest with wide eyes.

"What are you talking about? Why would you call me your mate?" I question, narrowing my eyes at him and his behaviour. What's he playing at? Is this another one of his attempts to break Rykan and I up? Because if it is, I won't let Rykan go so easily.

"I know that you can feel it. You're drawn to me," he says,

211

and when I don't deny it immediately, it's confirmed.

"Get away from him!"

The voice in my head suddenly speaking startles me, but I can't help noticing how different it feels to any other time it's spoken to me before. Before, I felt so disconnected to it, but now it feels as though we're one and that it's as much me as I am it.

"Get away from him. Don't let him sway you."

Although I'm confused, I heed the voice's warning, taking a step back from Cole, and he quickly notices, his eyes darkening at the act.

"Why should I get away from him?"

"He's trying to take us away from our love, Rykan."

"But he says he's our mate. Is he telling the truth?"

"It doesn't matter. The only mate I acknowledge is Rykan. I don't care for this weak wolf."

"So he's telling the truth."

The realisation has me gasping in horror. Cole is who Rykan was talking about when he tried to end things between us. Cole is my real mate. But I love Rykan, and nothing will change that.

"But I love Rykan," I admit, and instantly, a growl rumbles from his chest, the anger resonating through it, making me take another step back in caution, but he's quick, shooting his arm out and grabbing mine, pulling me against him.

"Don't tell me you love another wolf," he says, growling, his eyes turning a bright golden yellow colour. His wolf is now in control. Then his eyes land on my neck. "Did he mark you again? Did you two sleep together?"

His anger-filled roar has me flinching.

"Get away from him. He's going to hurt us."

"Let go of me," I say, struggling against his grip on me, but it only tightens to the point that it starts to become painful.

"Help me."

"I can't. I don't have control yet."

"That's it. I won't allow a man that's not me to touch you ever again," he promises, and when he leans down, my eyes widen in panic.

"No. Please no."

But it's too late because merely seconds later, his fangs come sinking into my skin. My immediate reaction is to scream at the top of my lungs. A pained howl escapes the voice inside me, and I cringe at the pain that erupts through-out my neck area. This doesn't feel like when Rykan marked me. This hurts, beyond belief.

Then I become numb, my body slumping against his. He retracts his fangs, staring down at me with satisfaction in his eyes. "Now you're mine."

A tear escapes my eye. Rykan isn't here, Cole is my mate, and he's now forcefully marked me.

What in the world do I do now?

To be continued . . .

ABOUT THE AUTHOR

I have lived my entire life Cape town, South Africa, where my life is run by 2 furbabies, a husky named Saskya and a cat named Stripey. I'm a hopeless romantic who dreams of having the kind of love I read and write in books. Coffee and music are my writing companions. When not writing, I like creating art with my hands and painting tiny canvases. My sister has never let me live down THE oven incident. In my own defence, she asked me to turn the oven on, she did not ask me to set the temperature. My only secret, my obsessions are known by those who know me best, but even they don't know about my solo karaoke sessions.